Two Women &

A novella by

A raunchy, racy story full of laughs mingled with a few tears, this is a poignant and highly entertaining story of two women's adventures pre and post-divorce. It celebrates friendship and their determination to discover what else life has to offer beyond marriage and kids.

This is a work of fiction. Names, characters, businesses, places, events and incidents are either the products of the author's imagination or used in a fictitious manner. Any resemblance to actual persons, living or dead, or actual events is purely coincidental.

With thanks...
Book cover by Samantha Parr -
https://www.facebook.com/SamParrArtandIllustration
Bev, Karol and Cyn, for their story line advice.

Prelude

15 January 2007

Alix and Suzi – Dogging dirt-bags & Casanovas

Steel, that's it, I'm steel. I'm rummaging around in the dark

cupboard in the hallway. *I know it's here somewhere. Ah-ha, got*

you! Snatching at the tube of expanding foam spray, I shuffle

backwards out of the space under the stairs, otherwise known as

the 'I might need you one day space,' and into the hallway. I shove

the can into my overcoat pocket and pull the hood over my head. A

quick look in the hallway mirror and then I leave through the front

door, muttering the same thing, over and over again. "Steel, I'm

steel," I say, as I start the car. About twenty minutes later I pull into

a quiet side street and switch the engine off. *Close enough.*

Leaving the car, I quick-march down the back streets of Stockport for about ten minutes, until eventually I'm standing outside Mike's house.

Cool as a cucumber and not caring if the whole street has stopped to watch me, I push open the garden gate, pull the can out of my pocket, and spray the edgings of the posts with the foam. Once the foam liquid starts to expand, I smile, pulling the gate slowly until it clicks shut. Within minutes, the gate is stuck, and no one is going to open it! As I walk back down the street there is a definite bounce to my step as I start singing, "Someone knocking on the door, somebody's ringing the bell, do me a favour, open the god damn gate!"

****

"You didn't!" Suzi exclaims.

"I did!" I answer. Grinning at Suzi's shocked face I take another glug of Bacardi.

"He'll go nuts if he realizes it was you."

"Well, then maybe he'll think twice before he tries to take someone to bed without telling them he's married with kids."

Suzi smiles softly at me. "At least you found out before anything happened."

"I know and I'd say thanks for small mercies but actually it was a big
mercy! Is every man on dating sites a lying scum bag?" Suzi shrugs back at me.

3

"I'd love to be a fly on the wall and see his face when he tries to open the gate."

"I didn't do it!" I say, in mock innocence. Suzi shakes her head and I laugh as I stand up, rather wobbly. I strike a pose, right hand on bent right knee, left hand on hip, and wink at Suzi.

"I didn't do it," I sing. "I didn't do it," I click my fingers. "He had it coming, he had it coming!" Suzi jumps up and throws her arm around my waist, and the two of us sing the prison line-up song from Chicago before we collapse onto the sofa laughing.

"Damn, but revenge is sweet," I sigh. Suzi smiles back at me with her soft, caring, worried-to-death-about-you, eyes. Tears roll down my cheeks and in a flash Suzi is next to me and hugging me.

"Why are all men such shits?" I ask between deep breaths and little sobs.

"I don't know, Alix. I've read *Men Are From Mars, Women Are From Venus* three times and I still don't understand how they're so different to us. I get that they like their dens, and like to chew a matter over before making a decision but I don't get how sex for them is simply an action, totally removed from any emotion." When I finally stop crying Suzi moves back into the corner of the sofa, pulls her legs up, and sits crossed legged before reaching for her glass.

"Thank God for Bacardi," she says and the two of us chuckle softly. After a moment of silence, I moan. "He was so handsome though!"

Suzi laughs. "All looks and no brains ay."

"No, all looks and no heart." I look at Suzi, and ask. "Why do we always fall for the shits?" Suzi shrugs her shoulders. "Not sure, but I guess it's the shits that make our hearts beat fast and make us go running for a Brazilian!"

"Whilst the good guys make us go shopping for house cleaners and batteries," I respond. Now the two of us are really laughing. It is our belief that you can spot the frustrated people who live in your street. On Sunday mornings, the men are outside polishing their cars and the women are in the supermarket, stocking up on house cleaning products and batteries. House cleaners to vent all their frustration into a bit of spit and polish, and batteries to re-charge the rabbit they use when no one is home, to *really* take away the frustration of being with a lazy arse partner.

For the last seven years, both Suzi and I have been seriously searching for that significant other; not someone who is perfect, but someone who is perfect for us. The time has flown by, both of us having serious (lasting longer than three dates) relationships with men who turned out, not to be 'the one'. And both of us have been on far too many 'first-night dates' than we care to remember. Time and time again the men we met on the internet turned out to be either married or already in a relationship. We were sick to death of all the liars.

Later, I wave Suzi off in the taxi, smiling at my petite, pretty friend until she is out of sight. Once the taxi goes around the corner I shut the door and return to the sofa. *Steel, I am steel.* But the tears roll down my cheek again and I know only one thing that helps the pain of loneliness, the numbness of too much alcohol. Reaching for the bottle, I pour myself a massive drink.

Hail stones crash against the bedroom window waking me earlier than I want to be woken. I open my eyes and look at the ceiling, groaning as the memories that being awake bring back: *and another one bites the dust.* I curl up into a ball to cry more tears. *Bloody hell, but where does all the water come from?* The tissue box has long been empty and I rip another strip of toilet roll off to blow my swollen, red nose. *This is rubbish, come on shake a leg, stop feeling sorry for yourself and move your bloomin' arse!* I obey my inner nagging. I clamber out of bed groaning as my feet touch the floor, increasing the intensity of the inevitable, headache. I pull on my dressing gown, slip on matching slippers and unsteadily, creep down the stairs, trying to fool my head into believing there is nothing but silence. For a moment I regard the Bacardi bottle and consider another drink. I pick up the bottle and shove it into a cupboard. *I won't give into self-pity today. Coffee, I need coffee.* I open the fridge and take out a tin from the door. Lifting the lid I inhale deeply. I make an extra strong pot then lean against the kitchen wall staring out of the window. The hailstones have turned to rain and the sound of it pounding on the window mingles with the drip-drip of the coffee machine.

I ponder about the unfairness of life. In the last seven years I had been on too many dates to mention. I'd had two meaningful relationships with men who were complete opposites of each other. There was Alan, who I had loved and who had loved me back, but he was married, and Bob who loved me and was single, but I hadn't loved him in the same way. I groan and pace the kitchen floor. *What's wrong with me? Why can't I be content with having someone who loves me? Stupid, stupid woman.* I had been married for twenty years to a man who had been cold and unloving, and I dreamt of being with someone who would wrap their arms around me and hold me tight. And now I had met such a man it wasn't enough, and I had let Bob go. I groan again and stop pacing to stare into space.

I had met Alan in the months leading up to the divorce, and at the age of forty, he had shown me that I was desirable, and had taught me how to enjoy sex. But it was Bob who was the most significant in my metamorphosis, and for that, I would always love him.

"What's wrong with me, Nan?" I ask touching a photo of my Nan on the wall. "What am I looking for?"

7

"You can't build your happiness on the top of someone else's unhappiness Alix," I hear my nan reply.

"Oh, don't start on me Nan," I reply. I pour coffee into a big mug, and then turn back to Nan's picture on the wall.

"Why can't you be like Suzi's nan? She says things like, 'having sex with a condom is like trying to eat a sweet with the wrapper on.' Why can't you say things like that?" There's no reply and I shrug my shoulders and shuffle into the front room.

Staring into my mug I am overcome with the certainty that I will never meet anyone and I will reach old age with no one by my side. "I don't know what to do, Nan," I whisper. "I don't know how to pull myself together. Why am I so self-destructive?"

"My little love," my nan's voice says, as clear as day. I close my eyes and imagine hugging her tight. "Write it all down, Alix. Let it pour out of you and then let it go." I open my eyes and look at the laptop. *That might work.* I go over to the table and sit down, open the laptop and put my password in. Clicking on Word, I open a blank page.

My future's a blank page.

Where to begin? When I was born? Gosh no, as that would take too long and be too boring. When I was a teenager? No, still boring. When I got married? Umm maybe, the kids had come along then and they're my world.

My marriage to George, hadn't been boring but it wasn't interesting enough to write about. What could I possibly say about someone who blushed when they heard a swear word, and who quickly switched over the telly if something raunchy came on? Someone who couldn't lie and hated injustice? Someone who was happy *just* being a mother and staying at home looking after the kids?

I know where I'll start. My corner lip turns up in a half smile. *I'll start after I asked George for a divorce.* He had been a right sod to me when he realised I wouldn't change my mind. But I didn't regret it, as my life changed when, at the age of forty, I had become a single mum. And amongst all the tears and moments of loneliness there had been tons of fun, hysterical laughter, and some great sex! That was when I had finally started to discover who I really am.

For months George had threatened to kill him-self and even the kids. He had sent flowers, chocolates and every present he could think of, but I had been waiting ten years to get divorced and so it was too late. *One thing I had learnt about myself, asking for anything was hard, but once I'd made my mind up, there was no turning back. I was steel. Cold, hard, emotionless. Well I have to tell myself that to get through one shitty thing after another.* Then, after only six months George met a very young woman (only a couple years older than our son) and started dating her. Some might think he was having a crisis, but seven years later, they are still together and happy, so divorce has been good, even for George.

Approaching the age of forty and completely broke, unskilled, and with no career experience, I cried myself to sleep at night worrying about how I would bring up the kids on my own. Those years had not been much fun and the stress had pulled me into depression. But then out of the blue I met someone who completely changed my life. I grin as I remember my first meeting with Suzi, and start typing possible titles for my memoirs:

Ponderings of A Sex-Mad Middle Aged Women..... DELETED

Lost and Found: A Journey of Discovery....... DELETED

Someone to Hold....... DELETED

Finding Someone Who Loves Me, Farts and All............ DEFINITLY DELETED

How to Dodge Dirt Bags and Casanovas...... DELETED

Two Women and Too Many Men... (I think we have a keeper!)

Chapter 1

Let's go back in time, to... June 1998

Alix

I can't stand it anymore... I want a divorce. I know George doesn't love me. Besides the fact that he never says the actual words, there are lots of occasions when he well and truly demonstrates it.

I stand on the kitchen sink unit, hanging the newly-washed curtains. Somehow on the way down my foot slips on the surface and I crash to the floor. I yell in pain and shock and immediately burst into tears. Mark and Cathy instantly charge down the stairs yelling "Mum, Mum". They find me crumpled up on the floor and rush over. Seeing the fear in their eyes makes me pull myself together.

"I'm fine," I reassure them, as they help me into the dining room to sit on a chair.

"Honestly, I'm fine. It's just the shock." They don't seem convinced as they hug me to death. "Pop the kettle on for me, Mark, I could do with a cuppa. Thanks love." Mark lets go of my arm and goes back into the kitchen.

"Shall we take you to the doctors?" Cathy asks.

"No sweetie," I answer, stroking her face. "Honestly, I'm fine, go back and play with your dad."

Mark brings me a cup of coffee and I smile at him. "Go on, you too. Thanks for the cuppa." I see the hesitation on his face and broaden my smile. He slowly turns and heads back upstairs.

My shoulders slump as I stare into my coffee. *He doesn't even care if I break a bone! He's still upstairs playing the Play-Station and hasn't even called down to ask if I'm okay.* Tears roll down my cheeks. I feel so lonely and rejected. *I'm steel.* However, even the old 'self-motivating' slogan doesn't help me today. I feel anything but steel right now. I feel worthless, rejected and unloved.

I move through the day in a fog, lost in my loneliness, despite the family being in the house. Mechanically, I cook and then serve tea, smile at the kids as they chat, and wash the dishes while they curl up on the sofa to watch telly. I can't wait for the day to be over.

"Going for a walk," I call out, as I head out of the back door. I walk a three-mile circuit, hands shoved in my pockets, eyes firmly fixed on the ground. On a 're-wind loop' my mind goes over every unkind word and action George has ever said and done. I'm not perfect, far from it, but I need something *more.* More than this loveless marriage, anyway.

Later that night, when everyone is asleep, I take the tub of sleeping tablets out of their secret hiding place and pour them onto the coffee table in front of me. I spread my hand over them pushing them around so I can quickly calculate how many there are. *There's enough.* I don't know how long I sit there looking at the pills, but suddenly, through the fog of isolation and detachment, I hear Mark snoring. I close my eyes. I love my kids so much. *I am steel.* My eyes flick open and I immediately shove the tablets back in the bottle.

I can't live like this anymore. It's hard to explain how and why I still feel lonely even with having two great kids. When I am battling through the darkness I become convinced they would be better off without me around. It's not logical and makes no sense. Yet that is what depression does to you. George and I have been married for twenty years but for the last ten I have wanted a divorce. If I'm *this* unhappy, I need to take drastic action, if not for me then at least for the kids. And just like that, after years of deliberating, I make my decision. In the morning I'm going to ask George to leave.

I can't sleep, of course. I lie on the settee and go over and over all the things I will say to him. There are two main reasons why I want a divorce: 1. I don't believe he loves me and 2. He has cheated on me at least twice. I remember vividly the fateful day five years ago, when he finally confessed to having affairs.

****

It had been a strange day. We had driven into Stockport to go shopping, and on the way home I suddenly heard this voice in my head saying, '*Ask him, if he's had an affair*'. The voice was so loud and clear that I looked at George in shock.

"Have you cheated on me?" I asked, in a very surprised tone. He didn't respond, just carried on driving without answering. I turned to look straight ahead, realising that his silence was confirmation to his adultery. When we arrived home, we put the shopping away together and I boiled the kettle. As I handed him a cup of tea I said, "You'd better tell me about it then."

It poured out of him, this built-up, guilt-ridden confession. I listened as he spoke about things, that if I'm honest, I'd already guessed. Then, as if that wasn't all bad enough, he told me about a prostitute he met.

"Remember that night you drove all over town looking for me?" he asked.

"The one when you came home at five in the morning?"

"Yes." He paused and I watched him in his discomfort, shoving his foot across the kitchen lino.

"Spit it out, George."

"We went to a hotel, and I must have fallen asleep because I woke up when I heard her shutting the door as she left. When I went into the bathroom to shower I found a message she'd left me." George wells up then, his voice breaking as his emotions take hold of him. I remain silent, waiting to hear the worst.

"She'd written on the bathroom mirror with lipstick, 'welcome to the aids club'." George lost it then and broke down. He'd put his cup on the drainer and leant over the sink crying. I hated him. I close my eyes and bring back that feeling. The room was spinning and it was making me feel sick. I remember that night so well. I had driven all over town looking for his car. When he'd finally come home at five in the morning I'd been standing on the drive waiting for him. I'd asked him where he'd been and he named a club. I promptly told him I knew he hadn't been there, and he replied saying he couldn't remember the name of the club he'd been to. I'd known he was lying.

I felt a rage inside me at his betrayal. But the thing that broke me was when he'd laughed at me that night. If that wasn't enough, when I asked him if he had been with another woman, he told me I was stupid. When you are told, often enough, that you are stupid you begin to believe it.

****

We had never spoken about his confession again. He had never asked me to forgive him, although for the sake of the kids I had tried very hard to. I hadn't wanted to get divorced until they were grown up, so I pretended everything was okay, when it clearly wasn't.

What had made me so bitter was that he had made me feel so little and stupid. Throughout our married life I had known our marriage wasn't perfect and I thought I'd been to blame, when now I knew that wasn't true.

The tedious night spent planning my epic, verbal revenge, ends at last and I go to wake the kids up. They grab some toast and do their usual dash out to college. I am just finishing washing the breakfast dishes when George comes down.

"I want a divorce," I say, as I dry the plates.

"Can we talk about it?"

"No."

"I love you, Alix." I put the plate in the cupboard and turn to look at George.

"I don't love you." To my utter surprise George breaks into floods of tears and tries to hug me.

"Get off," I yell, pushing him away. The only time he ever touches me is when he wants sex and I'm certainly not going to let him touch me now. He looks pathetic and I almost feel sorry for him, but suddenly years of rejection make me hard. I don't even need to tell myself that I am steel today, because I know it. I'm hurting him, ruining his life probably, but I feel no remorse. *God will probably never forgive me for this, but I can't take this life anymore.*

I turn and walk away from George, not wanting to spend another moment in his presence. I go into the utility room, empty the washing machine of its damp contents into the basket, and head into the garden. I'm still hanging out the clothes when I hear the front door slam. I shiver, finish pegging the washing out, and head back inside. Slowly, I walk upstairs to our bedroom. His drawers are half-open and I can see he's taken his things. I sit down on the bed in shock. *Was it that easy? No slanging matches, no putting me down or blaming me. All these years of wanting a divorce and he's left, just like that, without a fight! Just shows how little he cares about me.* I think I should be sad. Maybe cry? But instead a sense of joy floods my body. That he'd carried on having sex with me even though he thought he had aids was an unspoken confession to not loving me, not caring that he might be killing me too, leaving our children without parents.

"Oh Lord, I'm sorry, but I'm so happy." Now, I do start crying. I feel free, like a weight of chains has been cut off me. I feel light, ecstatic and full of hope for the future.

Chapter 2

August 1998

Suzi

"Mum?"

Okay, lunch boxes packed, tea in the slow cooker..., what is it, what have I forgotten today?

"Mum?"

I know they did their homework last night. I've got my sandwich, so what's wrong?

In a shout of frustration, "MUM!"

"What Tom? What is it?" Suzi snaps back at her son.

"You've locked Kim in the house."

Suzi looks out of the car window in shock to see an irate Kim yelling and waving in the front room window. *Oh shit.*

"Okay, easy mistake to make," Suzi shouts running back to the front door. "I did tell you to get in the car hours ago." Kim, red in the face from all the yelling, marches past Suzi in a state of complete indignation.

"Forgetting to lock the door is an easy mistake, Mother, but locking your child in the house is unfathomable."

"So sorry. No harm done though." Suzi answers, getting into the car.

"Just uncountable amounts of irrevocable, emotional damage."

"You do talk a load of cods wallop for a thirteen year old, Kim."

"You have noooo idea of the psychological damage you cause, Mother."

"Maybe not but I do know how to ground a back-chatting daughter." Kim gives an almighty huff and stares out the window in anger.

There is silence in the car for about twenty seconds, and then from the back seat, Tom states, in a matter of fact voice, "Confucius say, girl who has head up her own ass, have crappy outlook on life."

"Tom!" yells Kim, swivelling around in her seat, trying to whack him with her bag.

"Confucius also says, grandchildren are God's reward for not killing your children. So you both need to be really grateful for the fact that I think in the future I'd like grandchildren. Now turn around Kim and stop trying to pummel your brother to death." Tom sits straight and smirks at Kim. Kim huffs again and turns back to the window.

And so begins my day.

Suzi drops the kids off and then turns around and heads back to the A34. She is late again, and the ever-predictable traffic jam does nothing to calm her nerves. She pulls her make up bag out of her handbag and in-between inching forward and constant breaking she applies some eye shadow and a bit of lipstick.

An irritatingly long-time later, she pulls into a parking lot with a screech of the tyres, slams the door shut behind her, and dashes for the staff entrance.

"Hi Suzi," says a bald-headed, tubby man behind the counter, without lifting his head out from behind his newspaper.

"Please don't tell me I'm the last one in again," pants Suzi as she rushes past the security guard.

"You're the last one in again, Tiny." Suzi groans as she charges down the hallway. She flings her coat on a hook and manages to switch on the kettle before busting into the office.

There is a unanimous cry of, "Good afternoon Suzi," from all the staff.

"Bugger off you daft lot," Suzi quips. "I'm not that late." The boss's door opens and Suzi groans.

Tapping the face of his watch her boss calls across the office.

"And what time do you call this, half-pint? Did you stop to help deliver someone's baby again, or no wait, was it your son super-gluing his fingers together again?"

"Oh that's not fair. Tom's fingers hurt for weeks after he had them cut apart."

"Anyway, not too bad, you're only seventeen minutes late today."

"I'll make them up, although I can't today because it's Simon's work do tonight and he made me promise not to be late. So I'll make up for it on Monday, if that's ok?" Her boss burst out laughing.

"Suzi, you're the only person I know who charges full belt at life and *never* comes up for air. I'm going to buy you a snorkel for Christmas."

The day flew by in a moment and before she knows it everyone is turning off their computers and grabbing their coats. *I'll just finish this email before I go.* Forty-five minutes later, her boss appears next to her desk.

"Thought you had to leave on time today?"

"Yes, I do. Sorry about that, but it's a pretty important event for Simon."

"It's quarter past six Suzi," says her boss pointing to the wall clock.

"Oh fuck, fuck, I mean damn." Suzi flicks off her computer and runs down the corridor, yanking her coat off the hook as she goes.

"Night Suzi," says the security man, without taking his eyes off the telly.

"Night Keith," she calls racing out of the door.

The signal inside the building is rubbish and from the moment she gets in the car she hears her mobile ping, pinging with one message after another. She clicks her seatbelt on and sneaks a quick look at the phone, two missed calls from Simon and fifteen texts from Kim. Suzi groans and presses the contact button to call Kim.

"Where have you been? I've been texting you for ages. Why didn't you answer? Tom's playing up again… he's gone to play footie with his mates and dumped his bag and coat on me. I thought we were having spag bol for tea but Gran says you didn't tell her!"

"What's that Kim, Kim? Hello Kim? Sorry love, if you can hear me I can't hear you, bad signal, call you later."

"Mother!" Suzi presses the end call button and then instantly rings Simon.

"You're late, aren't you? Just this once I asked you to be on time. The speeches start at seven thirty for goodness sake."

"Hello darling, have you had a good day?"

"Just get here as soon as you can," Simon says and ends the call. The second the call ends her phone begins buzzing. She groans.

"Hello Kim."

"Can you hear me?"

"Oh yes, much better reception here. Before you start, let me speak to Gran, will you?"

"What are you going to do about Tom? It's not fair, he always gets his own way. And Gran is cooking stew, and you know I really don't like stew."

Suzi snaps.

"*I* will deal with your brother, you just take care of yourself. And as for tea, you're lucky you're getting anything at all. Do you know how many starving children there are in the world? Now let me speak to Gran."

"You always over react. I know there are starving children in the world but that doesn't mean I have to like stew."

"Your Gran, NOW."

"Hello love."

"Hi Mum, sorry about this. Let her go hungry if she doesn't want stew and I'll call Tom now and get him to go to yours straight away."

"It's okay love, he called me and asked if he could play football. He said he'd be here by six thirty so everything is fine. You go and get ready now and have a good night."

Suzi's entire being is flooded with gratitude for her mum.

An annoyingly slow, bumper to bumper journey home gives Suzi plenty of time to think of excuses should she miss Simon's speech. *Please, don't let me miss his speech.*

She's in and out of the shower in seven minutes. There is no time to mess about with dressing so the good-old-faithful, black dress will have to do, accessorised with silver high heels and jewellery. Dressed in four minutes flat. Dries and tongs hair a total of fifteen minutes. Make up, basic, no time for foundation. Five minutes later, all done.

Suzi looks in the full length mirror, to see what she's accomplished in half an hour, her best time yet. Five foot tall, big bust, tiny waist, long-blonde hair and delicately pretty, although she didn't think so. She loves this black dress, which clings to her body showing all her best assets whilst making her appear extra slim. She grabs her clutch bag, checks everything's inside: lipstick, keys, money, tissue, perfume, and mobile. Her phone has been pinging the whole time but for once she ignores Kim. She has to get to the Mere Hotel as quickly as possible or else Simon will be well cheesed off. As she heads down the stairs she hears the beep of the taxi.

The taxi drops her at the entrance to the hotel and Suzi rushes up to a member of staff in the lobby.

"Excuse me, but where are the Business Awards being held?" The guy she had spoken to smiles down at her and Suzi is caught off guard by his charm.

"I'm not too sure but if you ask a member of staff I'm sure they'll be able to help you."

"Oh, I'm sorry." Suzi's cheeks flush red.

"Not to worry, I'm often taken for the waiter in this dinner suit."

"No, no, I didn't think you were the waiter, I just don't have my contacts in and I saw you and I thought," Suzi's voice trails off. She *had* thought he was a waiter.

"Excuse me," says the gentleman to a passing member of staff. "Would you be so kind as to show this charming lady where the Business Awards are taking place?"

"Yes of course," answers Jean Luc, the hotel maître d. "This way please."

"Thank you," Suzi mouths with a grateful smile, to the handsome non-waiter, before turning and following Jean Luc, down the hall way.

The speeches have already started. *Please, don't let me have missed Simon's speech.* Suzi looks at the table plan and thankfully the Power Mills table is at this end of the room and easy to reach, near the back. She can see from Simon's pinched look that he is none too happy with her. She takes in a deep breath and exhales slowly to slow her heartbeat.

"Suzi, you look amazing as usual," says Tommy, Simon's business partner. Suzi smiles at him in relief.

"Thanks Tommy," she answers, slipping into the empty chair next to Simon.

"You haven't missed anything yet," says Katelyn, Tommy's wife. "Here, have some Champagne." Half an hour later Simon and Tommy are called up to receive their award for export contribution.

Suzi sits back in her chair and watches Simon, as he thanks his staff for their hard work. When he goes into details of the new ventures abroad she switches off and enjoys watching her handsome husband on stage.

The rest of the evening turns out to be fun, with loads of laughter, Champagne, and dancing. When the band announces last orders Suzi is taken by surprise. *Where has the evening gone and how on earth is it that time already?*

There is lots of hugging and kissing in the car park as everyone says goodnight and then they get into Simon's BMW.

"I didn't think you were going to make it in time," Simon says, after they had been driving in silence for a time.

"I'm sorry love, I was so busy at work. But I made it in time for your wonderful speech. I'm so glad I didn't miss it."

"Was it good then? Did I come across well?"

"Like a true entrepreneur darling." Ten minutes later Simon pulls the car over into a dirt track across a field.

"What's wrong? Why have you pulled over?"

"Nothing," Simon says switching off the engine. Before Suzi can say anything else Simon reaches over and pulls her face towards him. His lips hit hers hard and his tongue dives into her mouth.

"Oh," she whispers, as his hand goes up her dress and reaches her panties. He pushes them to one side and sticks his fingers deep inside her. "Oh," she says again, taken by surprise. She hasn't warmed up yet and is dry and it isn't completely pleasant. But he is kissing her hard and passionately and soon she is warmed up and moans in pleasure. She doesn't know if it is because she is tipsy and Simon is relatively sober but it seems like only a moment of kissing occurs before he lowers her chair, drops his trousers, and thrusts at her, trying to get inside.

She manoeuvres her hips slightly and uses her hand to guide him inside her. Simon grunts as he pushes deep. Suzi moans in pleasure as he fills her and moves her hips in time with his.

He must have been very excited because he comes within minutes, leaving Suzi wet, dishevelled, and slightly frustrated. *Guess it's nice that I excite him so such that he comes so quickly,* she thinks as she straightens her dress.

The rest of the drive home is in silence.

And so ends my day, she mused wryly.

Chapter 3

September 1999

Alix and the lothario

After the initial joy subsides, the overwhelming responsibility of bringing up the children on my own hits me. Fear grips, convincing me that I won't be good enough, that I will fail them and be unable to be both mother and father. Not only loving them, but also providing for them. How will I put food on the table and buy their never ending supply of clothes and shoes? How am I going to pay the bills? Fear takes its vice-like grip and squeezes my heart until it practically immobilises me.

I had been labelled with 'learning difficulties' at a very young age. I couldn't read or write for a long time, and when I did my grammar was awful. Later in life, I found out that I was dyslexic, but at school I simply thought I was stupid. My worst moment was when, at the age of eleven, I was told that as I couldn't speak English correctly I wouldn't be allowed to learn French and instead I would need extra English lessons. *Dunce, I am a stupid dunce. How the heck am I going to get a job and take care of my kids?*

I try my hardest to hide how I am feeling from Mark and Cathy. I smile and carry on as normal in front of them. I do not tell them what their father has done, or how he isn't prepared to pay maintenance towards their upbringing. I encourage them to continue seeing him while cracking up inside, allowing my hatred to build-up out of control.

I do the weekly food shop on my credit card with no idea how I am ever going to pay it off. As if not paying maintenance isn't bad enough, I return home from work one day to find that George has gutted the house of anything valuable. Not wanting the kids to see what he has done, I go straight to the shop and purchase a TV and computer on credit.

On the phone to Suzi later that day, I explained there'd been an offer on. I got five years free insurance and a free blue-ray player, so the TV was practically free. "We accountants know how to stretch the money," she'd replied.

I had smile at the kids when they come home from college and explain we have new things because Dad needs the ones we used to have. The cooker was broken and only the hob rings worked and the fridge-freezer hummed like an electric drill so he didn't bother to take them. He had taken half the furniture, crockery, and pans and left us the washing machine, so that his kids could have clean clothes. He also took every single photo we possessed. The only picture he left was one of us on our wedding day, but he had ripped it into tiny pieces and left it on the table.

Within weeks of asking for a divorce, I went to see a careers adviser. I took her suggestion and enrolled in college to learn something new. After completing a six month course I knew I would be bored simply data imputing, so very tentatively, I approached Stockport college business department. I felt nervous, I had to try and get a career. I wouldn't be able to support the kids on my current job of three hours a day butty making!

The head of the college was very understanding of my situation and assured me that 'in this day and age we used the calculator and I would be fine'. *Okay, I'm assured that if I don't get on with accounts I can switch my course, but at the same time I'm battling with the overwhelming knowledge that he's just had a dig at my age.*

My first day at college turns out to be one of the weirdest days of my life. *Blimey, I'm forty years old and back at school!* My insides shake all day as I think everyone is laughing at me, and then Suzi comes and sits next to me during lunch.

She smiles at me and begins talking away like the dearest of old friends, seemingly totally unaware that I want to hide and not talk to anyone. At first I had felt put out as I wanted to sit in silence and read my notes. I don't make friends easily as I never have anything to say to anyone. *Who would want to be my friend?*

But Suzi decided we would be study partners. To my amazement, the course came easily to me and I found satisfaction in being able to help my new friend. One day, Suzi and I decided to do lunch and from then on there was no going back. Suzi was naturally funny and quick witted and she'd made me laugh until my sides hurt. We became friends, despite the fact that Suzi was ten years younger than me, and we began to open up to each other and share our problems.

I told her why I was at college, and she explained that although she was in a well-paid job it wasn't satisfying, which was why she was back in college.

We went through some ups and downs together over the coming years, concreting our friendship forever. Amongst the pain, sorrow, tears, and the overwhelming fear of what the future held, we discovered laughter, different versions of love, and a pile of sayings we would continually throw at each other over.

'What doesn't kill you makes you strong' became the firm favourite.

Amidst the worry and stress, I had the feeling I had done the right thing. However, towards the end of the first year of separation, feelings of loneliness continued, so I went to explore AOL chat rooms.

I quickly discovered that these were not for me and instead started looking at groups and their message boards. I browsed frequently and I read all manner of things. Then one day, I came across a post written by a man called Alan who wrote about the complexity of women and how they were all different but all, in their own individual way, beautiful. Touched by his post I left a message for him saying how much I had enjoyed reading his notice.

That was when my life began to change. For five months, Alan and I instant messaged each other nearly every day. We talked about our days and what was happening in our homes. Alan told me he was happily married to Jo and had two grown up children like me. Every day, once my two had gone to bed, I rushed into my bedroom to switch on the computer. If for some reason Alan didn't come on I felt greatly disappointed. Alan had become my confident and adviser. He was interested in me and obviously didn't find me boring.

I poured out all the years of loneliness in my conversations with him and he listened. We shared our dreams, our likes and dislikes, and we laughed together so much. One day, I typed that I had overheard the girls at work talking about clutch-less knickers. He had laughed so hard he had fallen off his chair and Jo had come running upstairs to check he was okay. When he had finally stopped crying with laughter he told me that crotch-less knickers were, indeed, quite sexy.

Then one day Alan asked if we could meet. He confirmed he would stay at a hotel and that it would be nice if we could have dinner and talk in person. Alan's photo was on his profile so I could see he was slightly chubby and bald. I knew that if I had met him in person I probably would not have fancied him. However, we had become friends and after six months of talking I knew I had strong feelings for him. I had never put my photo up so Alan had no idea what I looked like.

I had grown up prim and judgmental. Rather awful traits I know, but if I'm anything, then it's honest. I vehemently believed that women who had affairs were the worst kind of women. They were home breakers and selfish beyond belief. I could never have an affair and be 'that woman.' But the thought of meeting my friend filled me with happiness. What harm was there in simply having a meal together? *Oh, what webs we weave, when we set out to deceive. And the worst deception of all, the one I spin myself.*

He lives in Cornwall and I live in Cheshire, so it wasn't as if an affair would work out anyway. So I agree to meet him for dinner.

Several weeks later, on a blustery day in March 2000, I drive into the car-park of the hotel in which Alan is staying. I feel sick with nerves and I am trembling. *What will he think when he sees me? What if we aren't able to talk in person as we do on the computer? What if someone he knows sees us? I know that's a long shot, but life is stranger than fiction they say, and for good reason. Besides I've never been able to stop my mind racing away with an entire list of highly improbable occurrences.*

Alan stands in the doorway waiting for me. Smiling, I walk towards him noticing the look of surprise that appears on his face when he clocks eyes on me, it's most definitely a good look! He shakes his head slowly from side to side as I stand in front of him.

"Wow," he says. I grin like a Cheshire cat and he leans in and kisses my cheek.

"I thought because you wouldn't send me a photo, that you must be," he hesitates for a moment, "well, not very attractive." I feel the heat rise in my cheeks as I blush. Alan seems to come out of his moment of surprise and takes control.

"Come inside, I've got us a table in the corner, by the window." He takes my hand and leads me inside. I'm impressed with him already, for taking charge.

The night flies by with the pair of us chatting like non-stop freight trains. He recites tales to me that make me laugh so much that tears run down my face. Without realizing it, I'd drunk far too much to be able to drive home. *Okay, in my defence I'm normally a Bacardi drinker and red wine has a way of getting me tipsy, even after only a glass or two, okay, large glasses but still ....* I notice the waitress clearing the tables and realize the restaurant is nearly empty. I glance at my watch.

"What time is it?" I ask. Alan smiles at me with laughing eyes.

"You just looked at your watch," he answers.

"But I don't have my glasses on," I giggle back. "I'd better call a cab I've had far too much to drink to drive home."

He reaches across the table and puts his hand over mine.

"Stay the night with me?" he asks, looking deeply into my eyes. "Nothing has to happen if you don't want it to, but stay with me." I take a deep breath. I want to stay but I know it would be wrong. I shake my head.

"I can't," I whisper. Alan nods and sits back in his chair.

"It's okay, I understand. I'll get your coat." I watch him go across the room to fetch my coat from the peg on the wall. By the time he returns, I have changed my mind. *Not all women are the same you know, but, if I have one very feminine trait then it's definitely, that I am prone to change my mind!*

A short time later I'm sitting on the bed looking at my hands. *I should go.* Alan puts his hand under my chin and lifts my face upwards. My eyes are swimming with tears, I feel so emotional.

Alan slowly kneels down in front of me. He reaches up and brushes my hair away from my face.

"I've really enjoyed getting to know you, Alix," he says softly. I smile.

"Snap," I answer. He leans in slowly and gently kisses me on the lips. I gasp, as the thrill of his touch sends tingles all through my body. I draw back from him, my mind is racing. *He's married, and I shouldn't be here.* Alan leans in again and kisses my cheeks, my forehead, my nose, and my mouth. His lips are soft, gentle, warm. Thoughts that he's a married man and that, I'm about to become the 'other woman' keep screaming in my head. *You're a cheap hussy!* Oh brain, please shut up! His hand traces along my leg, and I switch to, *thank heavens I shaved.* He's kissing me again, tender and searching. I kiss him back, a bubble of something crazy stirring in my stomach.

Oh God, he's married! This is wrong, I should stop. His hand slowly slides along my thigh going upwards. *I'm so glad I opted to wear my sexy little undies and not my comfortable, hold-you-all-in Bridget Jones knickers!* His hand goes beneath my undies and gently begins stroking my most private place. *Thankful, so very thankful, I didn't have oats for breakfast.*

He withdraws his hand and pulls me up off from the bed. In a blur of emotions, my 'non-stop' brain seems to have gone into hiding. The only thing I can hear is my own heavy breathing. Alan turns me around and starts undoing the buttons on my dress. The blur is gone and I freeze. Alan turns me around once more to look at me.

"What's wrong?" he asks gently.

"The lights are on," I answer, going red. Alan smiles tenderly at me.

"So? I want to see you."

"No, I can't do it," I shake my head and look down at the floor. Alan sits on the edge of the bed and pulls me down next to him.

"Why can't you?" he asks. I feel my cheeks burning and blush even more with embarrassment.

"I don't want you to see me naked."

"Alix, look at me." I slowly lift my head and peek at him from under my long fringe.

"You're a gorgeous woman with a sexy body and I'd love to see you, but if you're uncomfortable I'll turn the lights off." I nod at him and he gets up and crosses the room to switch them off. A soft pale light creeps through the curtains from the street lamp outside, just enough to see by. *Some men are just so clever, they know exactly what to say, to make a woman like putty in their hands. I'm not surprised that men do it, only that, not all men do it.*

"We don't have to do anything if you don't want to Alix." I sigh and nod, too emotional to say anything. Alan pulls back the duvet and climbs into bed with all his clothes on. He lifts up the duvet and puts his arm out signalling me to come in. I climb in and snuggle into his chest. He wraps his arm around me, covers me with the duvet, and starts talking.

There in the semi-darkness we spend the next few hours talking about all kinds of things, with Alan constantly teasing me and making me laugh. Eventually, I feel at home in his arms. After a little pause I lean up on my elbow, reach in slowly, and kiss him. My lips have been on his for only a moment when his right hand reaches up and holds the back of my neck, whilst his left arm moves around my body and squeezes me tight, pulling me in closer to him. I feel not only Alan's passion rise but my own, as he pushes his mouth heavily over mine, his tongue seeking the inside of my mouth. After a few seconds of heavy kissing the old fear of suffocating grips me. I push him away.

"I can't breathe. I'm sorry, but I just can't kiss like that."

"Okay, my sweet," Alan answers and immediately starts kissing my neck. No longer am I plagued by a million thoughts. I can only feel, as I undergo a kind of awakening. Feel his lips on my mouth, feel his hand on my breasts, feel a surge of excitement run through me like I've never felt before.

As Alan explores every inch of me I begin to tremble. My body is coming alive in a way I have never experienced before. I moan constantly, unable to prevent the sounds that come from deep inside me, erupting softly through my lips. As his lips touch my inner thigh my body jerks in shock, and an electric bolt runs through me. Alan stops and comes up to look at me.

"Are you alright?" he asks, concerned.

"Yes, I'm fine," I say, in a slightly high pitched voice. I feel too embarrassed to tell him I have long since passed *any* reservations about doing this. My mind might have scruples and principles but my body, obviously, has no such thing.

"It's just you're so jumpy," he pauses, "like it's your first time?" I laugh nervously; I can't tell him that I actually feel like it's my first time.

"Well, as I have two kids I can assure you, it's not," my eyes smile at him, longing him to continue. With a perplexed look he holds my gaze, as if seeking an answer. After a moment he raises his hand and gently strokes my face.

"You're so lovely," he whispers, then returns to kissing me, everywhere. I guess I should have been kissing him back, touching him and turning him on in return, but I am lost, good-and-proper, engulfed in a world of discovery and lust. Every now and then his hard member rubs against me, so I know he's excited too.

"I need to be inside you, Alix," he whispers in my ear. My legs eagerly part making room for him. The shock of the heightened passion I feel as he finally pushes deep inside me is only matched by the shock we both have, as we roll off the bed and land on the floor with a thump! We can't stop laughing and tears run down our face but eventually we find the middle of the bed once more, where we stay.

Despite the shock and laughter, Alan is still hard and when I am safely in the middle of the bed he pushes my legs apart so he can be inside me again. He positions himself and looks at me, demanding my full attention before slowly pushing inside me. I gasp and tremble as we completely join together, one in flesh and spirit. As Alan gets more excited he thrusts deeper and deeper inside me, and I feel as if my whole body has come alive. I arch my back and raise myself from the bed so I can hook my arms around his neck and gaze into his eyes. His head rolls back. "Oh fuck," he moans, as he finally releases his flood inside me.

We can't sleep, neither of us want to miss a minute of being together. We make love twice more during the night and each time I discover something new.

I once asked a friend how she knew when she had come during sex because I wasn't sure if I had. My friend had responded instantly with, 'If you're asking that question you've never had an orgasm.' One day on instant messenger I had shared that conversation with Alan.

That night together in the hotel, Alan had taken the time to not only explore my body, but to get me to explore it as well. I'd nearly died of embarrassment but Alan had been gently persistent, and in the end I had touched not only him but myself. That night would be something I would never forget and I will always be grateful to Alan for helping me to orgasm for the first time in my life, at the ripe old age of forty.

Christmas Day Dec 1999

I love Christmas and everything about it, the carols, trees, gifts, the turkey and all the trimmings. I spend a lot of time searching for gifts and love wrapping them. I especially treasure decorating the tree with the kids while we listen to Christmas songs and I drink Baileys, my Christmas treat. This was the first Christmas since we separated and stupidly, I asked George if he wanted to spend Christmas day with us. He had purchased a house around the corner, so the kids could see him whenever they wanted, but I knew they would prefer their dad to be with us for Christmas dinner.

At first it wasn't too bad, George playing with the kids in the front room while I worked in the kitchen. The first time I felt uncomfortable was when we exchanged presents. I hadn't got George anything, he had taken everything out of the house and I had put a noose of debt around my neck by buying everything new on my credit card.

But George had bought me a present. I open a box to find the most gorgeous necklace and I sit there staring at it for a long time.

George never got me gifts and when he did they were thoughtless. Now as I look at this beautiful intricate necklace I wonder why he'd not got me something when we were together.

"As this is my last opportunity to get a present I thought I'd get something special Alix, to make up for the times I never got you anything," George says.

"Thank you," I reply. "It's very pretty." I stand up and place the box under the tree.

"Right, Cathy, Mark, will you take John his lunch please?" John is an elderly neighbour that we take a roast to, whenever I make one. Cathy takes the plate of dinner and Mark carries the Christmas cracker (that they would pull with him) and the bag of home-made fudge along with a Christmas Yule log for his pudding.

With the kids out of the house I should have wondered what George was doing but it never crossed my mind until suddenly I hear my mobile ringing. Instantly, I run upstairs. After George had moved out I didn't want to stay in the same bedroom so I had moved into the tiny room and let Mark have the big one. I had purposely left my mobile under my pillow, out of sight. As soon as I see George trying to turn my phone off all flustered, I am furious.

"How dare you?" I scream at him.

"So you're having an affair! I knew that's why you asked me for a divorce." I snatch my phone out of his hand, shaking in anger, and

George takes a step back. In slow deliberate words that come out through clenched teeth, I snarl at him.

"You're the one who had affairs. I never started looking for anyone until after I'd asked you for a divorce. You have no right to question me or look at my phone. Now get out."

"What about dinner?"

"Get out," I scream. He takes the stairs two at a time and slams the door as he leaves. I sit on the bed shaking, overflowing with anger and hate. *God, help me please, I don't want to feel like this.* I look down at the phone to see what George has seen. There's a text from Alan.

'Merry Christmas babes, I miss you xx'

I type back, 'Merry Christmas to you too. Hope you're having a lovely day xx'. The kids come home laughing, so I go back downstairs to listen about their time with John.

"John says to tell you that you're an angel," Mark says.

"I'm afraid Dad has gone home as it was just a bit awkward for us." I expect them to be upset but they take it in their stride.

"In that case can we please have dinner in the front room? Star Wars is coming on soon," asks Mark, hopefully.

"No, not today, Mark." He doesn't argue back. During the week we eat in the front room watching the telly but Sundays and special days are for sitting around the table together, so we can talk.

****

I meet with Alan three more times. The last time we spent a long weekend together in Wales, which was romantic and lovely and I hadn't stopped smiling until our last morning together.

"I can't see you anymore Alix," Alan says, as we sit in the car driving back to Cheshire. I feel myself growing cold. I know that his words are right but I can't help the waves of sadness that wash over me.

"I understand. You love Jo and this cheating isn't right, I know that."

"No, you don't understand at all, Alix." I turn in my seat to look at him.

"I've been married for twenty-seven years and I love Jo, I do. Never in all that time have I ever wanted to leave her. She doesn't like sex, I get that, but there's more to marriage than sex and she has always meant the world to me, even though I've had the occasional fling." He pauses to glance at me, before turning back to the road.

"This is the first time I've ever wanted to leave her." We remain silent for a long time. I turn around in my seat and go back to looking out the window. I don't know what to say.

"I never set out to hurt you, Alix." I turn back to look at him.

"I know that," I say with a small smile, "but I'll miss you." Then tears start running down my face. *Why couldn't I have met someone who was free?* I try to stop crying, wanting to wait until I

44

was home and alone. *Where is my steel now?* When Alan pulls up outside my house I jump out, grabbing my bag from the back seat. Alan gets out of the car and walks me to the door.

"I'm sorry," he says, his eyes swimming with water. I can't speak so I just nod. I drop my bag on the floor and throw my arms around him. For a moment I don't want to let go but calm is coming back to me, and my chatty-brain is beginning to work once more. The steel is returning. I speak softly by his ear. "I will never forget you," I say. Then I pick up my bag and go into the house. He waits for a full two minutes, just standing there looking at the door and then slowly turns around and gets back in the car.

I deleted my AOL account that night and then meticulously deleted every one of his emails. Lastly I looked at my phone and read one of his text's. 'You were made for me.' I couldn't delete his messages one by one because I didn't want to remove the words that meant so much to me, so I deleted all the texts in the in box quickly before I could change my mind. Lastly I deleted his number. Sadness hung like a heavy blanket for a few days but then slowly I had started to smile again. I am steel. I wasn't with him anymore but Alan had helped me so much, he had built my confidence and shown me what good sex was all about. I would never regret meeting him.

The change in me was not only on the inside but reflected on the outside. I used to wear baggy tracksuit bottoms and huge men's shirts to hide myself away, I never wore make up and used to walk around the streets with my eyes firmly fixed on the floor.

Now I wear more fitted clothes, and make-up, but most significant I walk with my head held high. I am a woman, more than that, I'm a sensual women, who knows what I want.

One month later I received a phone call from an unknown number.

"Hello Alix." My heart jumped, it was Alan.

"Hi," I answered my mind already racing, why had he called?

"Alix, I have just been in the loft and got my suitcase down."

"Why?" I asked with a catch in my voice.

"I can't stop thinking about you Alix, I need to be with you, if you will have me I am going to leave Jo." There was silence on the phone as my thoughts went racing around my head. *I am steel.*

"I can't see you again Alan," I finally whispered, my voice catching in my throat. Silence again.

"Why?"

"Because my Nan is right, you can't build your happiness on the top of someone else's unhappiness. I can't let you leave Jo for me; I won't be responsible for that." Silence again.

"Are you sure?"

"Yes Alan, I'm sure."

"I love you."

"And I love you."

"Take care of yourself my little sweetheart."

"You too," I replied and switched off my phone before he could hear me crying.

Memories of Alan come back to me every now and again. I often touch the little silver butterfly necklace that he bought me. Not to remind me of Alan, but to remember that I have changed. Like the caterpillar that evolves into a butterfly, I would never be the same woman again, and that was thanks to Alan.

Chapter 4

March 2000

Suzi and the stereotype cheater

Suzi looked out of the kitchen window whilst she sipped her tea. Wives are always the last to know to know they say. *But I don't know anything.* For a couple of months now Suzi had 'felt' a change in the air. Simon wasn't quite how she always thought of him. He had become moody and sullen for long periods, and then like a light switch being flicked, he would be happy and bouncy and chase her round the house trying to kiss her. She didn't know where she stood with him anymore, and she didn't like it. On the surface everything looked the same, they appeared to be that lucky, happily married couple who had it all: love, kids, house and careers. She shook her head to come out of the contemplative mood. She was lucky she had everything, why was she looking for a reason to ruin it?

It was Saturday and it was Simon's turn to take the kids to watch City play at home. Normally, she would have enjoyed listening to the match on the radio but today she couldn't concentrate. She vaguely heard the crowd at the match roar and knew City must have scored. She switched the radio off. She didn't want to become that paranoid wife, who was suspicious of her husbands every move but, suddenly, she was running up the stairs. She pulled open the wardrobe doors and looked at his clothes. She hesitated, for the briefest of moments, and then she was diving through all his pockets searching for evidence.

Nothing. She sat on the bed and put her head in her hands. *What's wrong with me?* She felt herself welling up and wrapped her arms tightly around her tummy. *This is stupid, I'm being stupid.* She decided to make the beds as she was upstairs and found herself tidying up the bedrooms. She picked up their wastepaper bin and went into Kim's room to empty her bin into theirs. Just as she was about to pour Kim's rubbish into their bin, she stopped and put Kim's bin back down on the floor. She sat on the bed and put her hand into her bin to retrieve some sort of ticket out of it.

It was a bar receipt, from the Sheraton Hotel in London. Nothing odd about that, Simon travelled a lot for his company and she knew he had stayed in the Sheraton last week. What made her stare at the bill were the drinks on it, three pints of Stella and a bottle of Champagne. It was like looking at one of their drinks bill from a romantic night out. She felt sick as waves of heat swept over her. When the flushes started to subside she pushed the receipt into her jeans pocket and continued cleaning.

By the time Simon and the kids got home the whole house was pristine. Washing and ironing done, house fully hoovered and polished. Everything was spick and span.

Simon, as was normal, had picked up a curry on the way home and everyone piled into the front room to eat and watch telly. Suzi felt detached and watched the evening behind a fixed smile. She was counting the minutes until they would be alone. The moment she was sure the kids were asleep she pulled out the receipt and shoved it at Simon.

"What's this?" she barked. Simon looked at the receipt in surprise.

"It's a drinks bill?"

"Are you having an affair?"

"No! Of course not. Don't be stupid. Where did you get that idea from?"

"Three pints of Stella and a bottle of Champagne." Suzi looked at him, willing him to be honest.

"Are you nuts? It was a business meeting."

"A business meeting that involved Champagne?"

"We were celebrating the deal. Get a hold of yourself Suzi, you're being ridiculous." Suddenly Suzi's bottom chin started shaking as the tears came and the build-up of suspicion was released.

"Come here, you daft thing." Simon pulled her into his arms and kissed the top of her head.

"As if I would cheat on you, my little beauty."

"I'm sorry. I don't know what came over me. I think it's because you've been quite moody lately."

"Moody?" Simon pushes her away. "Moody?" He repeats. "Do you know how stressed I've been at work lately? No, you don't, you have no idea because I keep all the horrid stuff away from you, so that you can stay at home and play at the happy, I have everything, housewife. You have no comprehension how stressful things have been lately."

Conflicting emotions run through Suzi and she didn't know which one to land on. She wanted to confront him about the belittling statement of her 'playing at the housewife', but instead she went with the need to console him.

"What's wrong at work? I thought everything was going great, you've just won an award and the contracts are pouring in, I don't understand."

Simon sits on the settee with a sigh. "Everything is up in the air, nothing is concrete and we have borrowed money to the max and we need to make sure this next deal works or we could lose everything, that's why I'm going to Switzerland next week, to make sure they're happy with all the small print."

You're going to Switzerland? When were you planning on telling me that?

"How much money have you borrowed, exactly?" said Suzi, sitting on the settee next to him.

"Oh Suzi, I don't want you to worry about it, I will sort it. I promise everything will be okay. We just need to get through these next few months, that's all." She wanted to talk about it and find out what was going on but Simon pulled her into his chest and squeezed her tight. "I'm sorry if I've been moody, I'll try my best not to let work interfere with home life again." Suzi wrapped her arms around his neck and held him tight. *Funny, in my world of broke I'd never be buying bottles of Champagne, customers or not.*

"I don't want you to leave work at the office, I want you to bring it home and talk to me about it, just don't bottle it up." *Or I'll be putting that Champagne bottle where the sun don't shine.*

"I'll try not to baby."

Later on Simon made love to Suzi so tenderly, covering her body with kisses and gently touching her everywhere. "My sweet babe," he'd whispered into her hair, before he'd turned over and gone to sleep.

June 2000

Alix

It's 2am and I'm woken by the buzzing of my mobile.

"Hello?" I say, sleepily.

"You know how you told me, I could come to you any time I needed you?" It was Suzi. "Yes," I answer.

"Well, I'm at your back door now, can you let me in?" I spring out of bed and race downstairs. Opening the door I find a distraught Suzi, red, puffy eyes and an overcoat on top of her pyjamas.

"What is it?" I ask, grabbing her by the hand and pulling her in. "What's happened?"

"He's cheating on me." Suzi sobs, her chin wobbling. I pull her into the front room, take her coat and wrap her in the sofa blanket. As she flops onto the settee I place a box of tissues in front of her. I leave her for a moment to make her a cup of tea.

"Okay, tell me all about it." I say, passing Suzi a cup of very sweet tea. Suzi pours out the fact that her dick-head husband has been caught out. He'd told her he was going on a business trip, only for Suzi to find two flight tickets, one for her husband and one for some woman, and a holiday booking at a skiing resort.

"A leopard never changes his spots Suzi. You have to get rid of him."

"But, I love him. Since school he's been the only one for me. I've never even looked at another man since I met him. I don't understand why he's doing it. He says he loves me. We have two gorgeous kids and a lovely house. I don't understand why he needs to play around as well."

"Appreciating what they have, and understanding that it is enough, seems to be impossible for men, as far as I can see." I answer. "George could have had sex with me any time he wanted but he preferred to visit prostitutes instead. Go figure! I don't know why. He always told me he never cheated and then one day, out of the blue, he confessed to sleeping with a prostitute and thinking he had aids. Can you imagine how I felt? It made it absolutely clear that he didn't love me, because why would he have sex with me when he thought he had aids? You wouldn't do that to someone you love, would you? I battle so hard with feelings of worthlessness and the anger I have inside against him. I really, really try to forgive, but I just can't. Suzi you need to ask Simon for a divorce, don't waste years like me. Don't let anger eat away and destroy you the way it has me. Please do something before you waste ten years of your life."

"I don't think I could cope without him."

"Of course you will. You have to, because you have kids. You can't fall apart or give up, you have to get up every day and take care of them, and in doing that you will slowly work through it. One day at a time. And I will always be here for you."

"I'm not sure I would manage Alix, I'm not strong like you. I just love him so much I want us to live together and grow old and be happy." Suzi starts sobbing and I instantly move next to her and hold her tight.

"I'll be here for you Suzi, night and day. I'll help you I promise." I let Suzi cry until she is all cried out and the sobbing turns to soft muffles, then go back to the other chair.

"I'm forty, Suzi. I don't regret marrying George and I don't regret divorcing him either. But what I do regret is, not divorcing him ten years before I did. I wasted my life on him. I'm forty now and the thought of dating fills me with dread. I wish I could have got divorced when I was thirty, when I would have still felt young enough to have a chance at finding someone else. You're only thirty, Suzi, don't be like me and waste your life waiting for him to change. There is only one person in this entire world that we can change, and that is our self. You have to become strong, and you have to chase after happiness Suzi, it won't chase you." As I look at the friend I love so much, I know she will take him back. The 'idea' of a perfect marriage is in her soul. She believes when a man and a woman say "I do," that they should mean it, and it should be for life. One day I hope that I will be able to tell her about Alan, but I know I won't tell her any time soon. I fear the scorn she would have for me and I can't risk having her see me through different eyes. She's become my rock, my go-to support and my best friend. With a sigh, I go and fetch the spare blankets and pillows.

The next morning Suzi got up and went home before I even stirred. She'd been comforted but not convinced, she couldn't be hard like me. I wish I wasn't hard. I wish at the age of seven I hadn't had to convince myself that I was like steel. I wish my life could have been different. Then, if I had a penny for every wish I made I would be laughing all the way to the bank!

Suzi had a different upbringing and a different life to me. That meant she had a heart much tenderer than mine. Her innocence in life, in men, in relationships, radiated from her.

Simon ended up moving out; taking only one suitcase of clothes with him he had moved in with his lover. In the coming months Suzi lost so much weight everyone feared for her. A tiny five foot, delicate woman anyway, with the loss of weight she looked fragile. I tried my best to help her and to encourage her, but her world had fallen apart. Suzi came from a close-knit family, her parents and her siblings were all still with their partners. She felt like she was the only one who had a failed marriage, and it wasn't fair. Suzi was still convinced that there would never be anyone else for her. She felt like she had failed and she had no idea how she would manage without him.

It therefore, didn't come as a surprise that when Simon came begging for forgiveness, she let him come home. He told her he was sorry and that he couldn't live without her and the kids.

"A leopard never changes his spots." I reminded her. But she loved him and decided their marriage was worth fighting for. Everyone deserves a second chance right?

Chapter 5

June 2000

Alix - Peaking at forty

Shit, but I can't concentrate. It's Exam time. We're sitting in the large hall at Stockport college, where the blinds have been pulled to keep the blistering sun out, but the room is still sweltering. *I feel like a friggin' teenager, why the bloody hell did I decide to do this?* It's not the heat that's preventing me from reading the next question; it's the view of Paul's back in front of me. He's taken off his shirt and is sitting there in the tightest of white t-shirts, showing off his muscles to perfection. Those arms were wrapped around me so tight on the dance floor last week, and I know as we danced cheek to cheek that if Tim hadn't come and barged in, demanding I dance with him, that Paul and I would have kissed. *How am I to concentrate with him in front of me? He's not much older than Mark for goodness sake, get a grip! You're turning into a cougar!* Somehow, I do manage to focus. I put my head down and plough through the questions. One hour and twenty minutes later I'm finished, but looking at the clock I realise there is still an hour and forty minutes left. I know I should re-read the questions and make sure I haven't missed anything but I can't be bothered, I want to be outside and somewhere cool. I pick up my paper and, as quietly as possible, tip toe to the front to hand my exam in to the monitor. The tip toe walk to the back of the hall and to the exit feels like an eternity.

Once outside I sit on the wall and have a drink of water. Fifteen minutes later there is still no sign of anyone else coming out of the exam and I decide I've had enough of sitting on the wall. Nelson's Pub here I come.

As I walk to the bar I notice a sign that reads 'doubles for the price of singles up to 5pm'. *That'll do for me.* "Double rum and bottle of coke please," I say to the barmaid, whilst fishing in my overly large handbag for my purse. I sit at a table near the garden door, which is propped open, to catch the light breeze that is wafting in. I send Suzi a quick text telling her where I am, so she can find me when she comes out of the exam, although to be honest she'd probably have guessed. It's hard to believe the first year of college is finished the time has just flown.

This year had seen me transform, both inside and out. I used to have no confidence and was thoroughly lonely. Suzi had been instrumental in the change of my life and her bubbly personality had brought me out of my solitude and my shell. I'd never laughed so much in my life as I had done in the last year. Quite amazing really when you consider the fact that we were both going through the worst part of our lives. Our friendship was concreted in our determination to help each other through shitty times.

I'd been in the Nelson for ages and was just finishing my second double when Tim turned up. I watched him do a quick scan of the room until he found me. He grins, gives me a wink and heads over to the bar. I'm dressed in tight fitting jeans and a pretty top. I've even got make-up on! I've had my hair cut into a short bob and I've died it sandy blond. The saying that blondes have more fun is completely true. Whether it's because women feel sexier being blond, or because men think women who are bottle-blonde are out for fun I don't know. However, I don't just feel like a different woman to who I was before I met Suzi, I look like a different woman. Tim, complete with drinks, comes and joins me at the table.

"Thanks," I say, as he puts a rum and coke in front of me. *There's never any need for anyone to ask me what I would like to drink!* Fifteen minutes later Paul and a few other class mates arrive and join us at our table. Lengthy discussions about each question follow with various views on what was right and wrong. I keep quiet; I found the exam so easy it feels weird to listen to people talking about how hard they found it. Last to join us, ten minutes after the exam is finished, is Suzi.

"I know," she declares. "I finished ages ago but I couldn't stop going over the questions to make sure I had covered everything." I feel a bit of doubt now that is after all, what all the lecturers tell us to do. *Still, too late now. What will be, will be.*

"So we're meeting up at the Printworks then," declares Tim. Everyone agreed. A night of celebration in Manchester had been planned for a while. Suzi was driving us to the hotel in the city centre so she only had one drink in the Nelson.

"Come on you, time to go," she said. I stand up a bit wobbly and the room swishes around me, it's a moment before I can concentrate on making my way out of the door. Unfortunately, for me, there are three steps outside the door which I totally forgot about, my foot misses the first step landing on the second and then I'm falling as I miss the last step entirely and go crashing into the pavement.

"Oh my God, Alix. Are you okay?" Suzi asks, helping me to my feet. I know I have a goofy grin and all I can do is giggle.

"Oh," I say, sobering up slightly. "I've lost a nail." I hold up my hand so Suzi can see one of my nails has broken. "We'll fix it for you, come on." Most un-lady like I don't make it to the car before I am emptying my insides into the bushes.

"Think, I had best go home now," I say to Suzi, once we're in the car, before hiccupping.

"Absolutely not. We've worked hard all year, we've paid for the hotel, we have a pile of young men wanting to dance with us and we're going out." Lucky for me we aren't meeting up for ages. I manage to sleep for two hours before Suzi wakes me up with the smell of strong coffee. A cool shower, a sandwich and two headache tablets later and hey-presto, I'm ready to face the world again.

Later that night Suzi and I are watching Paul and Tim play pool.

"Say that again," said Tim.

"I've read that men peak in their twenties and women peak in their forties. So I find it a complete mystery why older men go for younger women. It's older women who know how to have a good time."

"Yes, but young women look good on the arm," says Paul.

"Oh thanks!" I reply. "Way to make a woman feel good."

"I didn't say they're better in bed," answered Paul, "you, can show me how good older women are if you want?" Paul gives me a wink. Suddenly Tim is next to me and putting his arms around me.

"Well, as I'm in my twenties and you're forty that means we're both peaking, so shall we have some fun?" I brush his arms off laughing.

"No thanks, I like men." I answer.

"We're men," Tim retorts, slightly put out.

"I meant to say, I like older men. You two are not much older than my son for goodness sake."

"So?" Paul says in all seriousness. I shake my head. *Oh, to have men my own age flirting with me, now that would be fun.*

"Anyone want to hear a joke?" asks Thomas, another young student from college.

"Aye, gone on," I said, hoping it would deflect the attention off me. Thomas comes up and sits on a stool next to me and Suzi.

"My mate, Zack, decides to have a party where all the guests are asked to come as different emotions. It's Saturday night and everything's ready for a *happy* party. The first guest arrives and Zack opens the door to see a guy all covered in green paint with the letters N and V painted on his chest. 'Wow, great outfit, what have you come as?' he asks. 'I'm green with NV' says the guest. Zack replies, 'Brilliant, come on in.' The next guest arrives and my mate opens the door to see a woman covered in a pink body stocking with a feather boa wrapped around her most intimate parts. 'Wow, great outfit, what have you come as?' Zack asks. She replies, 'I'm tickled pink.' Zack says, 'I love it, come on in.' Later the doorbell goes again, and Zack opens the door to see two Irish blokes, Paddy and Mick. They are standing naked on Zack's front door step. Paddy has his knob in a bowl of custard, and Mick has his knob stuck in a pear. 'What the hell is this supposed to be?!?!' Zack demands. Paddy replies, 'Well, Oi'm fok'n discustard, and Mick here has just come in despair."

Everyone around us starts laughing. As for me, for the first time since I was seven, I get uncontrollable laughter. This tiny bubble of amusement is inside me and refuses to go away. Every time I think I am back in control it creeps up on me and I am laughing again.

Laughing is so infectious. Before long everyone in the group is laughing at me. Suzi is wiping tears from her eyes, "Come on, let's go to the ladies," she says. I grab my bag off the floor and go laughing with Suzi across the room.

At 3am, after dancing until our feet hurt, we head back to the hotel. Both of us are carrying our heels, whilst the pavement isn't too kind to our soles it is much kinder than the stilettoes we had been wearing, so we moan and laugh, and make a slow amble back.

"Hi there," I say, plonking myself down on the fountain steps next to a guy with a bag of Big Issue newspapers. "What you doing out here, shouldn't you be at home by now?" The smell coming off the tramp is none too pleasant and I wish I could offer him a shower.

"I'll be kipping in the bus shelter later," he answers quietly.

"Sorry to hear that," I say. "Are there no rooms at the hostel tonight?"

"Dunno, don't like 'em, so I don't go."

"I don't have much money left I'm afraid," I say diving into my tiny handbag. I pour the change into my hands, only a few pounds.

"Here, will you get yourself some breakfast?"

"Thank you," he answers with a grin.

"Now, not cider you hear? Something to eat will be much better for you."

"Right you are."

"Come on, Alix. Time to go." Suzi offers me her hand, which I take and stand up.

"Look after yourself," I say to the guy.

"You too," he answers.

The encounter has sobered me up somewhat. I'm so lucky, so blessed. *God, bless him and keep him safe please.* Back at the hotel we wave at the night receptionist, head up a tiny escalator and turn left for the lifts. Suddenly, everything is spinning.

"Oh crap, I feel sick." I say, staggering backwards and leaning against the wall.

"Wait Alix, hold it. We're nearly back in our room." I moan. Suzi gets the room card out and waves it in front of a red button. A few moments later the lift doors open and Suzi takes hold of me to get me into the lift, but by the time we reach it, the door shuts.

"Damn!" said Suzi taking me back to prop me against the wall, before going back to swipe the lift control with the room card.

"Right quick," she said, grabbing me for the second time and heading to the lift. When the door shuts in front of us again we both bend double laughing. Back against the wall.

"Okay, third time lucky. Ready?" she asks, poised at the lift control. With laughing shoulders I nod back. She swipes the card dashes across to me and practically drags me into the lift, by which time we are both howling.

"Oh my lord," I say. "Can you imagine watching that on cctv?"

"We'll end up on 'Manchester behaving badly' at this rate, which just makes me giggle even more. A short, weaving-walk later and Suzi is swiping the key to open the bedroom door.

"Heaven is a bed!" I declare, as I charge across the room and fling myself on my bed. I fling a bit too much, slide over the duvet and end up falling in the gap between the two beds. All Suzi can see, she tells me later, are my legs sticking up, like candles in a cake. She manages to help me up and not long after we're washed and in pj's and snuggled under the covers.

"Suzi?"

"Yes."

"I need to change." There is quiet for a moment.

"In what way?"

"I don't think I appreciate how lucky I am."

"You're a lovely person, Alix, I don't think you take anything for granted."

"I'm tired of being negative. I have to forgive George and move on. You know I've come to realise that the failure of our marriage wasn't entirely his fault? In fact I probably think now that it was actually all my fault after all."

"Don't say that. It's not true. He was the one who cheated on you. He was the one who nearly gave you aids, for goodness sake."

"I know. But I've convinced myself since I was seven years old that I'm steel, and you know steel isn't only hard, it's also cold."

"You're nothing like cold, Alix. You're one of the most loving people I know."

"But I never wanted to be intimate with George. I never kissed him you know, never did one French-kiss in twenty years of marriage. I have to stop hating him, the only person it's hurting, is me."

"I'll never forgive dick-head."

"I hope, for your sake, that you do." There's quiet for a minute.

"Suzi?"

"Yes."

"If we end up eighty and still on our own, will you marry me?"

"Only if I can have the right side of the bed," she answers in all sincerity.

"Men come and go Suzi, but friends are friends forever."

"They are indeed, fluffy."

"Fluffy?"

"Well if you're going to be my 'bit-on-the-side' I need a pet name for you."

"I like it. Night Suzi."

"Night fluffy."

July 2000

Suzi and I are leaning on the table, looking at the screen on my laptop. The website open is the dating site, Match, and we're concentrating on the page that asks you to describe yourself.

"Well, I could be honest but if I put chubby, middle-aged, plain looking woman I don't think I would getting many 'Hello's'!"

"What have we said about putting yourself down? You're not any of those things."

"I'm forty."

"Well they say forty is the new thirty so you're still young and gorgeous!" I smile at Suzi, in gratitude for the fact that she has just lied through her teeth.

"So, how are things at home?" I ask. Suzi shrugs a little.

"Alright, I guess."

"You're sure he's still not cheating on you?"

"Well, I don't think I will ever be sure. How can I be? But, yes I'm pretty positive. Things seem to be going well between us. We talk about things a lot more, when he's home that is, he's still travelling around a lot for his job." My alarm bells ring loud and clear.

"And he stays in hotels?" Suzi looks at me and sighs, she knows what I'm getting at.

"Everything is okay, honest. The only thing that we really quibble about is college and you!" I didn't like Simon and I'm not very good at making my face behave, so I could well imagine he knew exactly what I think of him. Still I ask in a surprised tone, "Me?"

"Yes, he thinks you're leading me astray," Suzi chuckles. "He's right you know. I never used to drink alcohol at all until I met you!" I feign an 'I'm hurt' expression, before smiling.

"But you're glad right?"

"Gosh, yes. I think he's most upset about the fact that I'm not automatically the nominated driver anymore."

"What's he got against college?"

"He says it takes up too much time and that I'm not doing the stuff I'm supposed to do, good-enough anymore, as I split my time up too many ways."

"What he really means is that he hates you spending the night out with me."

"Maybe, but I'm not going back to the person I was before the break, Alix. I have to have more in my life now, I can't let him and the kids be my entire reason for living." It was the right thing to say but in my heart I questioned how much she really meant it, or whether actively encouraging nights out with me was her way of keeping him on his toes.

"I just want you to be happy," I say, moving in for a quick bear-hug.

"Anyway back to this post, beautiful, voluptuous woman seeks handsome stud." We discuss in length what we should put but in the end, I have an honest, 'normal' profile.

Three weeks later I receive a long email from someone called Bob. I looked at all his photos and read his profile about ten times. He seems quite nice, very normal looking and sounding. I decide to write back. For the next eight weeks Bob and I correspond with each other a few times a week, Bob asks me several times, if I want to meet up and I finally decide I had nothing to lose, and say yes.

It's Saturday afternoon and my son is about to drop me off at the pub where I've arranged to meet Bob.

"And you'll come back in two hours to pick me up, earlier if I text you?"

"Yes, Mum. Go and have fun." I smile at him nervously as I climb out of the car and take a deep breath. *Lord, but I feel nervous.* The sun is shining and the breeze is warm, so I'm wearing a pretty, yellow summer-frock and matching high heels. I had a strong Bacardi whilst getting ready but my hands are still trembling

70

slightly. I tut at myself. *Why on earth am I so nervous?* It was only a drink in a pub and if we didn't get on I wouldn't have to see him again. Mark had chatted cheerfully at me all the way here and tried to put me at ease. I peered through the open window of the car.

"You'll keep your phone on all the time, in case I text you?"

"Yes Mum, and if I don't hear from you I will be back at six to pick you up." I smile at him and straighten up. I'd only taken a few steps away from the car when I hear someone call out my name. I turn around to see Bob walking towards me.

"I thought I would wait in the car park for you, so you didn't have to walk into the pub on your own."

"Oh thanks," I answer smiling at him. *That was thoughtful.* The next two hours fly by quickly. We sit outside in the garden in the shade of a large, old oak tree, Bob drinking fruit juice whilst I stick to my good, old-faithful, Bacardi. Within a short time I feel comfortable with him and find myself relaxing. I'm quite surprised when my son rings me to say he's back in the car park.

"I could take you home later if you wanted to stay a bit more?" Bob asked, as I got up to leave.

"Thanks, but I need to get home now. Thanks for offering though." Bob walks with me back to the car park and when we reach the car I stop and turn to him.

"Thank you for a really nice afternoon." Bob leans in and kisses my cheek.

"You're welcome, I had a lovely time. I'll call you then, if that's ok?" I smile up at him.

"Yes of course, that would be lovely."

"So?" Mark asks, as soon as we're driving away. I look out of the window for a moment before answering.

"He seems like a lovely guy but I'm not sure he's for me, I think maybe he is too old fashioned for me." Mark laughs out loud.

"You mean he probably won't want to go clubbing with you?" I chuckle.

"No, he definitely wouldn't want to go clubbing with me, but then, what forty something man would?"

"I know a few who would go clubbing with you Mum, there's Chris at the hotel for one, he's always asking after you, wanting to know how you are and has said he would love to take you out sometime, he parties hard so he would take you clubbing."

"Well flattering though that is, Chris also smokes too much pot to be my cup of tea, but thanks for letting me know love, it's nice to know you're fancied."

"Loads of men fancy you Mum". I look at my son and feel a wave of gratitude and love for him wash over me.

"Well I know that's not true, but thank you anyway." Mark just shakes his head to indicate that there's no telling me.

The following Saturday I meet Bob again, this time we go out for an Italian meal, my favourite type of restaurant. I wear another feminine dress, and this time a bit more make-up and my favourite perfume. The Italian waiter takes an instant shine to me and is over the top trying to impress me, which makes me merry and as I chat to Bob I know my eyes are sparkling. Most of the time I feel drab and dowdy, but this evening I'm having a "good day" and I feel happy and confident. I know that Bob is taken with me, I can always tell, *well I think I can,* when a man is interested in me. Three and half hours later Bob is walking me back to my car.

"Are you sure you wouldn't like to come home for a coffee? I only live five minutes away from here."

"No thanks, Bob. But I look forward to our day out next Saturday, been ages since I've been for a drive in the country." I give him a soft smile and stand on tip toes to reach up and kiss his cheek.

"I'll pick you up at eleven then," he said, and I smile at him.

"That's a date, see you then." As I drive off, Bob waves at me from the pavement. Just for a moment as I look in the rear mirror at him I wonder what I'm doing. He isn't my type. I like strong decisive men; men who take control. Bob's like a large teddy bear, lovely, gentle and sweet but not really my cup of tea: so what am I doing then? I think about it all the way home. *I'm not doing anything wrong* I tell myself as I stand in front of the mirror later.

I'm just seeing if we could work, that's all. The feeling that I'm doing something wrong won't leave me, and several times I reach for the phone to call him and cancel, but each time I put my hand back down again. He might just be good for me. Calm and quiet to my stress and mess.

The following week at eleven o'clock precisely, Bob rings the doorbell. I fly down the stairs and open the door.

"Come in," I chirp, "I'm almost ready. Take a seat in the front room I'll be down in a mo." I leave him to it and race back up stairs. I throw my lipstick into my satchel, pull my pumps on and take one last look in the mirror.

"The best of a bad job," I tell myself as I look in the mirror. My heart is racing. *I'm not doing anything wrong,* I remind myself, *I'm just going to find out if we could fit together that's all.*

We drive to Arley Hall and walk around the gardens. I love this, looking at the beauty of nature. I love woodlands and little walkways that look to be little secret paths. I feel happy. When Bob takes hold of my hand I don't knock him away, it feels comfortable. We have cappuccinos and the best cheese cake I've ever tasted in the little cafe on the estate. I can't stop smiling at Bob whilst he chatters away at me, and I'm glad that he doesn't seem to be bothered by the fact that I'm not a big talker. I always think that what I have to say bores people and over the years I've simply taken to saying as little as possible. *Well, except when I am with my girlfriends, and then I feel free to be myself and never shut up!* But in the company of strangers, and especially men I tend to keep my thoughts strictly inside my over-active brain.

"Do you fancy coming back to mine for a take-away and a movie?" Bob asks on the way home. I don't hesitate.

"That'll be nice."

We opt for chicken kebabs and a rom-com. A couple of lovely hours later the film comes to a stop and I have a good stretch.

"Thanks for a lovely day Bob, but it's time to go home now." Bob moves close to me on the sofa and picks up my hand and squeezes it.

"Don't go home, Alix." I look at him and my brain instantly goes into overdrive and I don't know what to do. I throw several conversations around in my brain and then finally one line wins. *We're both single and grown up and we're not hurting anyone, so why not?* I nod at him.

"Okay," I say quietly.   He doesn't hesitate and leans in straight away and starts kissing me. I kiss him back for a moment and then the normal feelings of suffocation start to crush my windpipe and I pull back from him slightly and kiss his cheek. He stands up pulling me gently to my feet and then leads me upstairs. We go to a room which is obviously his.

"I'll be back in a minute," he says leaving me alone. I run my eyes over the old-fashioned furniture and the big double bed and suddenly feel like a teenager; I sit on the end of the bed before I fall over with nerves, not too sure what to do with myself.

"Oh," said Bob, with obvious surprise. As I turn I see him making a hasty retreat from the room, totally naked. I turn my head forward with a snap, heat flooding my face.

Oh god, I don't think I can do this. A moment later, Bob comes back into the room with his trousers and shirt back on.

"Are you okay?" he asks. I nod back at him; I can't trust myself to speak my throat feels so dry. He leans in and kisses me very gently on the lips. Softly his hand reaches up and caresses my neck. His fingers move through my hair and I instantly moan. *I guess I'm just a wanton woman.* After a moment or two I begin to relax and Bob sensing that slowly pushes me down on the bed. There was no rush. Bob takes his time, tracing his hands up my legs, over my stomach, gently brushing his hand over my breast and down again to my legs. My body is a distinctively different anatomy to my brain. No matter what ten-to-the-dozen thoughts and objections my brain throws about, my body reacts on its own accord. Shudders run through me as Bob's hands explore. My mouth decides to act on its own for suddenly I hear myself moaning. *Be quiet you hussy!*

Before I really know how it has happened Bob had removed my clothes and I lay naked on the bed. He kisses my neck, shoulders, then down my arms and to my fingers. His fingers gently trace down the outside of my legs and then back up the inside, coming to a halt an inch away from my private garden. I can't help it and arch my back; he uses the moment to slip his fingers inside me. *Oh God*, my brain screams as my mouth lets out a low soft moan. His fingers are going in and out of me now, in, circular movements, out, back in. I can barely stand it. My juices are flowing and his fingers are wet, still he carries on. *Take me*, I yell inside my head, *oh please take me*. But Bob has other plans. He starts kissing my body again. He kisses my neck and my shoulders and moves slowly down until his tongue finds my nipples. He flicks his tongue over them and I moan and move under him. His tongue plays with me until my nipples are erect and then he's gently sucking. A good proportion of my breast is in his mouth and he sucks hard, all the time flicking me with his tongue. Shudders go through me. My juices flow and spill down my leg. He moves downwards once more, kissing his way over my stomach until he arrives at my, now wet, opening. With a firm hand he pushes my legs open and I almost come then, at the confidence and strength in which he handles me.

Once my legs are open he uses his forefinger and thumb to pull back the vulvas and his tongue flicks over my clitoris. *Oh God, oh God,* I'm literally screaming inside my head, but they are to be my last thoughts as my body takes over and completely shuts down my mind. I feel horny, it's washing over me in waves the more and more he works on me. When he finally pulls away and comes up to my face, I am panting and shivering with desire. I can't open my eyes but I feel Bob as he comes to kneel between my open legs and slowly pushes his hard member inside me. I moan in pleasure and arch my shoulders to come up to his mouth to kiss him. He let me give him a few fever pitched kisses then pushes me down again. He moves his hips, very slowly, so that he can push himself deep inside me and I let out a moments yelp as he hurts me, instantly he pulls back slightly and then starts entering me again and again, in a slow, rhythmic pattern that begins to drive me crazy. He builds in power and speed until he seems to lose control himself and then finally, on a huge shudder, he is filling me.

We lay afterwards for quite some time catching our breath. He wraps his strong arms around me and pulls me in close against his chest. I sigh and before long I am falling asleep. I wake some time later with Bob trying to move me without disturbing me. My eyes flicker open.

"I just need a drink of water," he whispers. I move myself so that he can get up. He returns shortly with two bottles of water. I'm trying not to smile at the fact that he has just strolled through his house entirely naked. *What confidence.* He opens one of the bottles and passes it to me.

"Thanks," I say, taking the bottle. It would be things like that, the opening of the bottles for me that I would always look back and remember with a smile. He's a true gent.   When I put the bottle down I turn on my side to look at him. He grins at me like a little boy.

"Was it okay?" he asks. A trickle of laughter bubbles out of me and I shake my head.

"I don't want to sound rude or anything," I answer, "but I was just *not* expecting that!"

"Why?" he asks, with a puzzled look on his face.

"I don't know, I had this picture of you as shy and quiet and well you are quite the Casanova!" Now it's his turn to laugh.

"That's a good thing right?"

"Oh, God yes, that's a good thing."

I have to remind myself why we broke up! Gosh, but it was great sex. Twenty years I had been married and I'd never come once. I feel like the first half of my life was lived as a sleeping shadow. Now, in my forties, I'm alive and I'm soaring high like an Eagle.

Chapter 6

Dec 2000

Suzi and the Christmas gift

It's freezing! Suzi dashes from the car into the Garam Massala, winter boots, coat, hat and gloves don't stop the icy wind making her shiver.

"Nearly ready Suzi be about five minutes," calls a tall, slim handsome man behind the counter, as she walks in.

"Thanks Vivek," Suzi smiles back. She removes her gloves pushing them into her coat pocket and then takes a seat by the window and stares outside. It might be freezing but the snow is beautiful, a white Christmas, just too perfect to be true. She smiles with happiness at the Christmas tree on the walkway; you could just see the twinkling lights under the heavy layer of snow.

She'd just had one of the best days ever. Simon had taken the day off work, a rare thing, and all four of them had put the tree up together, wrapped presents and sung Christmas songs all afternoon. It was the first time Simon had ever helped put up the tree and the kids had enjoyed themselves so much. And to finish off the perfect Christmas Eve she was here to collect the traditional curry tea.

She almost falls over on the way back to the car as her foot slips on the path, for a moment she is toppling, waving her arms, trying to gain her balance and prevent the dinner ending up in the snow.

"Got you." Suddenly, a strong pair of arms has caught her and is straightening her up. Her hair had blown across her face and she tries pushing it to one side with the back of her arm as she has bags in her hands.

"Here." The 'accident preventer' brushes her hair to one side with one of his gloved hands.

"Thank you, you just saved Christmas Eve for me," said Suzi with a laugh. The stranger smiled at her. "You're welcome," he replies, and then he lets her go and goes on his way down the path. *I know you?*

As she drives home, she tries to recall how she knows the stranger. Suddenly the memory of the 'not' waiter at the Mere Hotel comes back to her and she realises it was the same man. *How funny, what a small world.*

"Grubs up," she calls, as she came in the hallway kicking her boots off. She's hanging up her coat before it strikes her that something is wrong. Simon's suitcase is in the hallway and the house is too quiet. She walks slowly, a dread gripping her heart in the tightest of holds, as she enters the front room.

Straight away, she can see that Kim and Tom have been crying. Simon is standing in front of the fireplace.

"For the children's sake I need you to behave like an adult."

Suzi looks at Simon as he speaks to her; his deep blue eyes are cold and hard.

"I've just explained to them that I can't live here anymore, that you and I are unhappy and it would be best for everyone if I move out." Suzi's legs buckle and she sits down hard on the settee, an explosion has just gone off in her brain.

"You've picked her over us then?"

"No, there's no one else I just need to have a different life, one where I don't feel strangled in routine."

"Liar!"

"I'm going. I'll call you next week to arrange visiting the kids." Kim sobs and runs to Simon throwing her arms around his waist.

"Please don't leave us Daddy," she sobs. Tom is crying hard but doesn't move from his chair. Suzi watches as Simon tries to unclasp Kim.

"Are you just going to sit there or are you going to see to your daughter?" Simon snaps at Suzi. In a trance like motion Suzi stands up and opens her arms for her daughter to come to her.

"Aren't you going to stop him?" Kim screams at her. When Suzi doesn't answer Kim runs out of the room and up the stairs. Suzi follows Simon into the hall, where he picks up his case. As he opens the door Suzi says.

"It's Christmas Eve." For just a moment there is a look of regret in his eyes and then the door closes and Simon has gone: after throwing a grenade and destroying all their lives, and leaving her with all the aftermath.

Suzi crumples to the floor. She can't help it, she knows she should be comforting the children, but she needs to let the pain out. She moans loudly as the pain she feels in her stomach twists and cramps, and then she's wailing. The months of built up tension and suspicion, and now the pain of complete abandonment and rejection, wreck through her being.

"Mum," both Kim and Tom run to her and throw themselves upon her. Kissing her and holding her tight crying hysterically with her. Suzi doesn't know how long they all sit there crumpled and broken on the hallway floor but eventually she realises that Tom is shivering.

"Come on," she said, "Get up. We're going to Gran's."

They put their shoes and coats on and each go into different rooms turning off the lights and making sure that the doors and windows are locked. Suzi goes into the front room; she bends double with pain when she sees the tree and all the presents wrapped up under it. *Not now.* She leans down and turns off the tree lights, then retreats into the hallway. They pile out of the house and as Suzi shuts the front door the last thing she sees is the bags of takeaway curry on the hallway floor.

"Alix?"

"Hi Suzi, can't believe you called me today, Merry Christmas."

Suzi bursts into tears.

"What's wrong, what's happened?"

"Can you come home?"

"Not really Suzi, I'm in the Lakes and we're preparing Christmas dinner. What's happened?"

"He's left me."

"What, oh my God, the fucking shit!" I burst into tears. "I'm sorry Suzi, I'm so sorry. How are the kids?" Suzi just sobs on the other end of the phone.

"Are you at your Mums?"

"Yes," Suzi sniffles. "I've just come upstairs to call you; Mum is watching a film with them. I couldn't hold the tears in any more. I'm trying to be strong for them Alix, but it's so hard. I feel like my whole world has been ripped apart. When are you coming home?"

"The day after tomorrow, I'm sorry Suzi I can't leave now, all the family are here and I have to drive my mum home when it's finished. I will get to you as soon as I can. Are you going to stay at your mums?"

"Yes. I can't face going home to the Christmas tree and everything. The kids won't open their presents they say they don't want them." Suzi completely breaks down and the two of us sit with the phones to our ears and listen to each other whilst we cry. After a while Suzi sniffs.

"I had best get downstairs and watch the film with them."

"Okay. Well you be strong. Remember you're better off without the lying scumbag, you can build a better life for yourself now. It's not the end of the world, I *promise* you it's not. You're a beautiful, kind, loving woman and any man would be lucky to have you."

"Any man except Simon."

"That shit-face will come to realise one day exactly what he has lost, trust me. I love you Suzi, and I'll be with you as soon as I can."

"Love you too, Alix."

What kind of man leaves his children on Christmas Eve? A man who doesn't care that forever more his children will feel that Christmas is a time of dread and upset instead of joy. Only a man with no compassion would do that.

Simon had come home after his first affair and Suzi had forgiven him. It had taken a few months for the edginess to wear off but then she had thought they were going to make it and be okay again. Eighteen months he'd had, to make his mind up to leave again, and he had chosen Christmas Eve to do it. There was no coming back from this, no forgiveness available for the hurt he caused the kids. Suzi was devastated that he could hurt the children so much. She also felt completely unloved and undesirable. Her self-esteem had become null-and-void.

As Spring moved in, Suzi who couldn't eat, had lost a dreadful amount of weight for a second time, not that she really had any to lose in the first place, and she became gaunt.

She needed my help and the support of her family. The moment when she asked for a divorce, the fighting began in earnest. And with fighting a strength is found, and maybe a little too much un-forgiveness, but somehow this kind of strength was what Suzi needed to get her through. One day at a time. After all, what doesn't kill you makes you stronger, right?

And so here we both are, on anti-depressants and leaning on each other. Not knowing how we're going to manage as single parents, or how we'll pay the bills and bring up our kids on our own. But one thing holds us up through everything, friendship.

Chapter 7

May 2001

Suzi and the honest guy

"Are you sure?" I ask, for about the tenth time.

"I'm sure. I don't see why he should get to start a new life and move in with another woman, while I'm supposed to sit at home on the shelf and twiddle my thumbs!"

"I didn't say you should sit on the shelf, it's just that we need time to heal and I think dating at a time when we feel so vulnerable isn't really a good idea."

"I'm going on a date Alix, not asking someone to marry me. I'll be fine. I just want to have some fun, and some grown up company." Suzi stops drying her hair to look at me. I have one of those faces that you always know exactly what I'm thinking, and right now worry is written all over it.

"I'm lonely, Alix." I throw my arms around Suzi and squeeze her tight.

"I know," I whisper.

An hour later I'm dropping Suzi off at the pub. "Just text if you want me to come back for you," I say smiling as Suzi gets out of the car. I watch her walk across the car park to the pub. *Oh, I hope you have a good time.*

Suzi goes straight to the bar so she doesn't appear to be looking for a stranger. Whilst she waits for her drink she checks her phone. Just then a text pops up from Mike ... I'm behind you! She spins around to find Mike standing behind her, grinning.

"I'll get that," he says to the barman, handing over some money.

"Thank you."

"You're welcome. Come on, I've got us a cosy table." Suzi follows Mike over to a table in the corner. She feels a wreck. Her hands are visibly shaking and she feels sick. *Only having a drink* she tells herself as she sits down.

An hour and two drinks later and she feels much calmer, in fact she is quite enjoying herself. She is definitely attracted to him and he seems to like her. They laugh a fair bit and Mike can't believe she's a real City fan and seems to really enjoy her analysis of the last few games.

"Don't suppose you would like to come round to mine for a coffee would you?"

"I'm sorry, I don't drink coffee."

"Oh, okay," he says, obviously disappointed.

"I drink tea, if you have any of that?" Mike laughs.

"Yes, I've got tea."

In the taxi on the way to his house, Suzi remembers Alix's lectures. *Nothing more than a kiss and never, ever, go back to their houses on a first date.*

"Tea or wine?" Mike asks.

"Tea, please."

"Okay, go in the front room and make yourself at home I won't be long." Suddenly Suzi begins to feel that Alix might be right. She suddenly doesn't feel comfortable and wishes she hadn't come. She takes her coat off and sits bolt upright on the sofa. She uses the time to look around. Everything is nice and normal and quite comfortable actually, not what she would have expected from a single guy.

Back with the tea they both started talking again and as they chat she feels herself relaxing. Before long, Mike has moved close and starts kissing her. Her thoughts go into overload-rationalization about her ulterior motives for being here. She kisses him back and realises straight away that she wants to do more than kiss. After a few minutes, Mike pulls away from her and picks up his cup. After a big drink he puts it down again and turns to her.

"When my wife left me I was really lonely. I threw myself in dating and must admit I had several disasters of which I'm not proud of. But that was nearly three years ago and I know exactly what I'm looking for now." Suzi drops her head, a rejection is coming she can feel it. "You're a lovely woman Suzi, you're so beautiful and really, *really* sexy, and to be honest, I would love to take you to bed right now." Suzi looks up at him and smiles, maybe not the rejection she's dreading. "But you're not ready. You've got to give yourself time to heal before you do this, otherwise you're just going to hurt yourself badly."

"I just want some fun, that's all. Is that so bad?"

"No it's not, but it's also not what I'm looking for Suzi, I'm searching for my life partner so I can settle down."

"Well, how do you know that's not me unless we date for a while?"

"Because we are in different places and you need time to be single before you start looking to be a couple again."

"Best call me a cab then," she says slightly sharply.

"You're a cab."

"Ha ha." She can't help but smile though, as rejections go that was a pretty decent one. On the way home in the taxi she does nothing to stop the tears that flow down her cheeks.

Mike seems like such a nice man, why didn't he give me a chance? We might have lived happy-ever-after for all he knows.

The next morning Suzi drives straight round to my house, to tell me all about it.

"You know what Suzi, there is no such thing as happy ever after, only happy right now. That's what we need to search for. Not Mr Perfect, but Mr Perfect for me, and not to think of him as our happy ending, but to appreciate it when we're happy."

"I know, but Mike seems like such a lovely man I'm sure we could have been happy but he didn't even give us a chance."

"I know and that makes me like him all the more, he's a good guy, someone who has been hurt himself and who not only doesn't want you hurt but is protecting himself. And quite frankly, when someone is still upset over their ex, then they're a likely candidate to hurt us."

"I wouldn't have hurt Mike, I wouldn't hurt anyone."

"No, not on purpose you wouldn't. We're all on different roads, Suzi, we just need to find someone who is travelling the same way as us."

"Ugh?"

"When timing is perfect you'll meet someone who gets you, because he's in the same place."

"So back onto the dating sites it is then?"

"Don't you want to wait a little while first?"

"No, I don't. I only have one life and I want to live it. I won't sit at home feeling lonely and sorry for myself, when dick-head is out there having all the fun."

Suzi is to become relentless and I have to admire her. Her drive to find someone, not perfect, but perfect for her, is applaudable. There would to be some tears, some laughter and some great sex along the way to finding Mr Right-now.

Chapter 8

July 2001

Alix and Suzi do coffee

One Saturday afternoon I'm gazing wistfully at Mr Muscles when my jeans start to vibrate. Unfortunately for me, I'm in the super market, Mr Muscles is an oven cleaner and the vibration only my mobile. I pull the phone out of my pocket.

"Hi," I say, to be greeted by giggles. Suzi has to wait until she has stopped giggling before she can speak.

"Where are you, we've got to talk?"

"I am contemplating using up my pent-up energy by either cleaning the oven or spring cleaning the bathroom, and I'm hard done by to choose between the different Mr Muscle bottles." Suzi laughs.

"I'm here too," she answers. "In the whipped-cream aisle, meet you at the tills in ten." The whipped-cream aisle indeed, she's teasing, whipped-cream because whipping turns her on and cream is what she pours over her tied-up men, so that she can lick them all over! It's code for, sex life is good.

A short time later finds us sitting in the café next door.

"Okay then, let's have it," I say, leaning towards Suzi with a warning, "but remember we are in public, pre-water shed, so indoor voices only."

"Well, you know how I'm no good on red wine," Suzi says with a wink.

"I do."

"To be fair I did warn John that after two glasses of red wine I'm not accountable for my actions. So when he arrived at mine with two bottles of red in his hand I knew, how does that song go? There may be trouble ahead!" Both of us smile knowingly into our coffees then Suzi continued.

"As you know this was the fourth date, wink, wink! It was all hot'ing up nicely when he stopped in his tracks and said he had something to tell me. Instantly I thought, oh no not another guy into wearing women's knickers." I nearly choke on my coffee and grab a napkin to clean up. I raise my eyebrows at Suzi. "And?"

"Alas no, not as simple as that. He started by telling me he had been in a car crash and was an amputee."

"Oh no," I groan, feeling bad now for having jested at him.

"Oh yes," said Suzi, "he lost his left leg from the knee down."

"Oh dear!"

"No, but that's not all. You know those dreadfully expensive stockings I bought last week? Well the Velcro on his prosthetic leg caught the side of mine as he took his trousers off and ripped them! I don't mind but they cost me twelve pounds bloody fifty! It gets worse! When we finally made it into the bedroom he took his leg off, because it gets uncomfortable, and just as we were about to get to it, the dog crept in then ran off with his leg!" The two of us give up all hope of being quiet and laugh hysterically.

"There was this awful thud-thud-thud as Muffin ran down the stairs with it. I was mortified and tried leaping out of bed to chase her, but somehow got myself caught in the duvet, and not only do I go crashing to the floor but I bring John with me! I'm there fighting to get out of the duvet to chase the dog, I'm saying, sorry-sorry, like a trillion times and he just bursts out laughing at me."

"Well that's good; at least we know he's got a sense of humour."

"True, but I felt dreadful. I told him I had to chase Muffin before she started to bury his leg and he told me not to fret because, fortunately, he had a spare at home."

"So you weren't the only one that was legless then," I giggle. A lot of the nearby tables have started to empty, only one old lady remains and I smile as I watch her adjusting her hearing aid. *The better to hear us? Now I'm not saying that the old woman is nosy, far from it. We probably remind her of being young, she is smiling after all. But adjusting her hearing aid like that is something my mum always does when she thinks she can get a clearer sound. That will be Suzi and I one day, adjusting our hearing aids to listen to our tales.*

"So, that aside, did you have a good night?" I ask, turning my attention back to Suzi with a 'tell me the truth' stare.

"Oh rather!" Suzi answers. "If I was to give him a number from a scale of one to ten, with one being dick-head and ten being an Adonis, well I would have to give him 3 – for making me come, 3 – for being a gentleman, 1- for effort and 1 for a good choice of wine!"

"Wow, an eight that's quite impressive, in fact with our past record that makes him almost perfect. So do you think you will want to date him for a while or is this just fun?"

"I don't know yet, he's very sweet and he does make me laugh but he seems a little restrained for me."

"You mean you've had him tied to your bed already?"

"Twit, didn't need to, he's only got one leg he couldn't possibly run anywhere, besides putting the metal ankle cuffs around a man whose only got one ankle just seems a bit harsh, although I wouldn't really have had any complaints from him, as his gag meant he was unable to talk!"

"You didn't get the hand cuffs out on the first night together?"

"No, I'm only teasing; we'll wait till date five for that."

"Do you remember the time you left the handcuffs on the bed and Jack's mum came to spring clean?" The two of us start laughing again.

"He never did introduce me to her although his dad always asks if we're still dating. Oh that was funny, can you imagine your mum coming in to do you a surprise favour and finding all the bondage stuff lying around, not funny really, but made me feel like a naughty teenager again."

"Do you miss Jack?"

"I do, we went out for six months you know and we got on really well, but he's just one of those men whose really frightened of the word 'relationship.' I know he thought a lot about me but he just couldn't bring himself to give up his bachelorhood lifestyle. Shame because I wanted to take care of him so much I'm sure if he had let us we could have had a special relationship." All the humour is suddenly gone. Jack is one of *those* blokes who doesn't want any responsibility, okay fun-time guy, but faints if you suggest, *hold on just putting my finger to my lips because we have to say the dreaded word in a whisper,* relationship!

"He's just a worm Suzi." Both of us pick up our coffees and drink in silence for a moment. He wasn't a worm really; we both knew that, he was just honest about what he didn't want. Men, why were they so hard to understand?

Suddenly I'm chuckling. "Do you remember that song about worms?" I start singing the first line very quietly and Suzi joins in.

"Men might be worms but we do need our garden aerating now and again." We chuckle away together.

I head home feeling cheerful, I love Suzi so much, despite all our woes, when we're together we're able to make each other laugh and somehow our troubles seem further away. *A problem shared is a problem halved, they say, and it's very true.*

When I get home I take my big mug of coffee and sit at the garden table. I smile as the sun pours down into my little bit of heaven and warms my face. I look around my courtyard garden, filled with happiness. The tulips and daffodils are coming to life for another year, breaking through the soil in my huge pots, reaching for the sun, determined to blossom again. I am filled with a quiet determination to be like them, to push through the yuck and reach for the sky. One day I will share this bit of paradise with someone I love, and who loves me just as much in return.

Chapter 9

Aug 2001

Alix and the Dom

It comes as a shock to me, when quite by accident, I find myself emerging as a submissive. This sexual discovery makes me feel like a moth transforming into a most exotic butterfly, bursting with colours of desires that have long lay hidden within my soul.

The film 'The Secretary' is responsible for my revelation. A cinema fan I go to the pictures two, sometimes three, times a week, and most of the time I go on my own. I am on my own one day as I walk into an empty cinema to watch The Secretary. I'm mesmerised by the film but can't figure out why I'm enjoying it so much. I watch it three more times that week before the realisation of the appeal awakens me up to my carnal instincts.   As I watch James tell Maggie what to do my inners contract and a yearning grows within me. I'm a strong, and most definitely an independent woman who prides herself on her strong *(steel like)* character, so I find myself amazed at the growing desire inside me to be told what to do. Timing can sometimes be perfect, because it is a few weeks after the release of this film that I started dating Bob.

One Friday evening at Bob's house I'm browsing through his books and films in the front room, whilst he puts the kettle on in the kitchen. As my eyes trace along the many rows I suddenly stop, there on the shelf is The Secretary. Quick as a flash I reach up and grab the book and rush into the kitchen. A spark of sudden excitement is inside me as I look up at Bob and ask.

"What do you like about this book?" Nervous at first Bob hesitates to explain what he likes but I push and eventually he admits that the spanking gets him rather hot under the collar. This is the beginning of a new world, a new me, and a great sexual relationship.

Bob, as it turns out, is a dominant lover. Once he realises that I want to learn about the world of being a submissive he couldn't be been more excited. He takes me upstairs and shows me his trunk (not a little box, a full size 'let's move house' trunk) in his bedroom, that is safely under lock and key and full of toys. With eager, trembling hands he leads me into the world of a submissive. He is wonderful, never pushing, always asking, and slowly, like Maggie in the film, I shake off my grey persona and explode with a thousand slivers of sexual discovery.

Bob starts by putting leather handcuffs on me and tying my hands behind my back. He's so gentle, always checking I'm comfortable and ensuring me he'd never do anything I don't want to do. My trust in him grows and as the weeks pass Bob introduces more and more things into our sexual play. We watch a burlesque program together one day and the eroticism and sexiness of the tight basque appeals to me. I tell Bob I quite fancy a basque myself. The next day we go shopping together at Ann Summers. I'd never been in the store before and find myself surprised at how many 'normal' looking people, and mostly women at that, are shopping in there. We find the black corset the woman had worn in the program and Bob buys it for me. I can't wait to get home and try it on. That night Bob ties me into the corset so tightly I nearly fall over, but the feeling of being constricted sends my insides berserk. I feel so horny and sexy.

Bob plays with me as if I'm a delicate doll, I feel desired and wanted and the whole thing is exceedingly intoxicating. More and more, as he realises I won't reject him, he begins to tell me about the things that arouse him. He reveals his biggest fantasy to me one day and without hesitation I tell him we should act it out the following Saturday.

It's a lovely evening for a drive in the country and it's almost dusk when Bob arrives at my front door to pick me up. I climb into the passenger seat and Bob leans across and kisses me. His right hand rests purposely on my thigh, not as an act of intimacy but checking that I'd complied with his orders and that I'm wearing my vintage suspender belt and stockings. Feeling the outline of the suspender strap and the raised metal clip at the end Bob smiles, I know he is pleased, not only because he loves suspenders but because I'd obeyed. He glances down at the bodice of my dress and traces his finger along my décolletage before pulling back my dress and glancing down. I'm wearing the quarter-cup bra that he told me to put on. Satisfied, he clicks my seatbelt in and starts the engine.

We'd decided earlier that we would drive to the woods at Alderley Edge but on the way Bob pulls into the car park of a quaint little pub. We're going to have a drink as we wait for the last traces of daylight to give way to the darkness of the night, which is needed for what we have planned. The pub is quite full and we sit on bar stools as Bob orders our drinks. He looks around at all the, mainly upper class, patrons sipping on their evening drinks and looks at me with heavy eyes. I know he's aroused by the fact that none of them know what I'm wearing or what I'll allow him to do to me in a short while. I let my hand momentarily trace over his trouser front and feel that he's going hard, I smile as I imagine him inside me and let my hand linger on his leg.

After finishing our drinks we set off for the woods and drive down some dark country lanes until we find a very quiet location.

We park down a small track that leads into the woods. Reaching the barrier Bob stops and switches off the engine. My stomach lurches. The gentle brush of his hand along my thigh sends shivers running down my spine. All week I've been building in excitement with anticipation of this evening. Reluctantly Bob breaks away from me. It's time to get me ready. The week's planning; texts, calls and nightly whispers down the phone have all been for this. Now we're in the woods and I'm about to put my complete trust in him and succumb to his secret fantasy.

Our eyes are locked as he clicks the cold steel handcuffs around my wrists. My heart is pounding fast, I have never felt such lust before, he's done nothing outwardly sexual all evening but from the moment he opened the car door to me I had been excited. Bob lifts my hair so that he could put a collar around my neck. He padlocks the collar and then clips a chain to it. He gets out of the car and comes around to my side and opens the door. He uses the chain to pull me out of the car and leans towards me, I close my eyes thinking he's going to kiss me. Instead, he ties a scarf around my eyes. A slight tremor of fear ran through me. *I do trust him, I do. Don't I?*

I hear him close the car door and then he's putting metal ankle cuffs on me. When's he's finished checking the cuffs he pulls the chain and leads me slowly into the woods. I stumble slightly and his hand reaches out to steady me. *I am safe, aren't I?* After a short while he stops and lets go of the chain. I can hear him moving around, the leaves crunching under his heavy step, then he's with me again, gently manoeuvring me until I'm kneeling on the blanket. Slowly he bends me over until I'm kneeling on all fours. He lifts my dress and the breeze caresses my legs and backside, making me shiver. He pauses for a moment and I know he's taking in the view of my vintage suspenders and seamed stockings.

I jump slightly as his hand touches the top of my leg. Thrills ran up and down my spine as his hand slowly moves up to my backside. With a slow controlled movement he pulls my French knickers down to reveal my peachy bottom. He rubs one cheek and then the other; I hold my breath and can't help but tense. Slap! Small and slight it doesn't hurt at all but sends a shock of awakening through me and I moan in pleasure. Bob slaps one cheek and then the other, again and again until my cheeks begin to glow red and warmth radiates through to my inners until I'm soaked. Each slap becomes harder. My moaning has been getting louder with each slap and Bob knows when I reach that point that makes me explode, he thrust his hand between my thighs and pushes his fingers inside me, he moans himself when he feels how wet I am. I know the realisation that he can give me so much pleasure turns him on. He sits back and I hear him undo his zip. Bob is a tall, chunky guy and his member reflects his build. I realise he is rock hard when he uses it to stroke my rosy cheeks. It's time to be inside me.

He enters me slowly, his hands gripping my waist as he pulls me back towards him, at the same time pushing himself forward. Then very, very, oh-so-slowly, he pulls out. *Oh the pleasure.* The sensations inside me burst out like fizzy sherbet making my inners contract. He doesn't last long, the excitement is too great, and he releases himself inside me on a wave of shudders. As soon as he's finished he turns me over and lies down beside me. His hands are shaking as he traces his finger across my face, and then he pulls me in and gives me a crushing, tender hug.

Chapter 10

Sep 2001 to May 2002

Alix and the nice guy

For a while everything seems great between us. I would spend a lovely weekend with Bob and then go back to my house on Sunday to be alone. This works for me as I need my space, my empty time when I don't have to talk to anyone. My time of complete peace and quiet. In fact I am quite aware that I am just as happy coming home to an empty house as I am going to his.

After we'd been dating for only five weeks Bob turns to me on the settee one day and says. "I know this is too soon." *Oh no,* I yell inside my head, *don't say it.* "I know you don't feel the same way yet, but I have to tell you. I've fallen in love with you." Crash. Everything in my head is crashing.

"Don't worry; I don't expect you to tell me you love me, I just want you to know that I want you in my life." I can't answer. There is this clamp that appears when I am nervous and it grips my vocal cords so tight I can't open my mouth because I don't know what will come out.

We spend the next few months not mentioning love again but it's always hovering in my thoughts. We are walking through Tatton gardens one day and Bob is chattering away. As I look at him I am overwhelmed with guilt. *Why can't I love him? Isn't this all I have ever wanted, my entire life? What's wrong with me?* I squeeze his hand tight and smile at him, but that other voice in my head has started, my constant, nagging voice. *If you don't love him let him go, it's not fair he could be looking for someone who deserves him.*

That night I want to finish the relationship, I want to tell him but in such a way as not to hurt him, *does such a way exist?* But I can't do it. I can't open my mouth and voice what's going on inside me. So I hug him and go home to write a goodbye email. His email back to me is painful to read because although I don't want to hurt him, I have. I email back that I'm sorry.

For the next three months I go to work, return home, sometimes meet friends for a coffee or my kids for a trip to the pictures and that is it. Three months of quiet. Then one Saturday afternoon there's a knock on the door.

"Hi," I say, in complete shock, as I look at Bob.

"Hi," he answers, "going to let me in?"

"Of course." I open the door so he can step in. My hands have started shaking slightly. *Why is he here? And why is it so good to see him?*

"Coffee?" I ask.

"Yes please." *That buys me a little time to get myself together. What on earth is wrong with me?* Coffee made and back in the front room we sit down on opposite settees and just begin to chit-chat. After a while he puts his cup down and looks at me.

"I guess you're wondering why I'm here." I nod, easier than talking. "I just wanted to check that you're okay and it seems you are." I nod again.

"Daft really, but you see I've met someone." My heart sinks and my stomach convulses.

"Oh," I finally say. "That's good. How did you meet?"

"At a rock concert, she was in the seat next to me."

"That's a lovely way to meet someone." *What's wrong with me?* I can feel tears building up. *Not now. Pull it together. Damn, damn and blast.* The tears start. Of their own accord they start flowing from the corners of my eyes down my cheeks. I smile at Bob.

"Sorry," I say reaching for a tissue. Bob jumps up and sits on the settee next to me taking my hand.

"Why are you crying?"

"I don't know, I'm sorry, I don't know." Bob puts his hand under my chin and makes me look up at me.

"Tell me." I shake my head.

"I can't tell you."

"Why not?"

"Because, I don't know how to put it into words."

"Try." I shake my head; the lump in my throat is threatening to strangle me. Bob looks at me for a long hard moment then gets up.

"I'll be back tomorrow at twelve o'clock to take you out for lunch." I nod.

Sunday turns out to be a lovely sunny day and I surprise myself with how much care I go to, in an attempt to look as nice as possible. Twelve prompt Bob knocks on the door. Before I step out, I look at him.

"What are we doing?"

"We're just going out for lunch as friends." Relief washes over me, he doesn't think that we're getting back together.

For the first twenty minutes we just chat about our kids and jobs like good friends. Then, without taking his eyes off the road, he drops the bomb.

"Now, you're going to tell me everything and I'm not taking you home until you have opened up and let it all out." My heart goes crazy fast in my chest and my hands start to tremble.

"There isn't anything to say," I hear the shakiness in my voice.

"Bollocks, that's crap Alix, and you know it and I know it. Start talking or this is going to be an awful long drive." For half an hour we sit in complete silence.

"Do you know what tensile strengths are?"

Bob looks at me with a puzzled look on his face. "No."

"It is the maximum stress that a material can withstand whilst being stretched or pulled before it breaks." Bob flings me another puzzled look.

"Steel has a very high tensile strength. I didn't know that when I was little, in fact I only looked it up on the internet recently. But from the age of seven I have told myself I am steel." I'm quiet for a while as I try to put into words all the tied up confusion that's inside me. Bob remains silent with his eyes firmly fixed on the road.

"I don't want to talk about what happened, but from that time I have found it very hard to talk about anything at all. I don't enjoy small talk. You need to know I am a completely messed up person and you're better off forgetting me." Bob doesn't take his eyes off the road or answer me, which surprises me. But a few minutes later he is pulling into a car park.

"Let's have lunch." I look at Bob and can't help smiling. I know he'd heard me but he wasn't going to press me. My feelings for him increased dramatically in that moment. Lunch is beautiful and must have cost Bob a fortune, the whole time he keeps chatting at me like nothing in the world was wrong. By the time we get to take our coffees onto the veranda I am completely relaxed.

Back in the car we don't talk, I assume he's taking me home and sit up straight, more than a bit irritated, when I realise we're back at his house.

"I need to go home Bob, I need to get things ready for work tomorrow."

"Just one coffee Alix, and then I'll take you home." I'm afraid he's going to ask me questions and I start bringing down the steel shutters. I'm right. No sooner do we sit down on the settee when he looks straight at me and says, "You need to tell me." I feel my jaw tighten into its stubborn stance.

"I want to go home," I say standing up. Bob stands up next to me.

"Sit down Alix, you can take as long as you like but you are going to tell me."

"No," I say heading for the door. "If you won't take me home I'll get a taxi." Bob takes several quick strides and stands in front of the door with his arms spread wide across the doorway as he looks down at me.

"You're not going anywhere until you talk to me." Tears of frustration escape and I wipe them away in anger.

"Let me pass," I snap, trying to prise Bob away from the door.

"No." After a fruitless attempt to push him aside I give up and go back to the settee. Bob comes back to the settee and takes me in his arms. He holds me tight for a moment and then sighs.

"You don't have to look at me. Just lie against my chest whilst I hold you and tell me what happened." I can hear his heart beating fast in his chest, dear man. I don't know how much time passes but eventually I start talking.

"When I was seven years old I lived in a small fishing village. Everyone knew everyone, including the local bobby, so I was safe. I was crazy independent and went missing some times for hours on end, must have driven my poor mum crazy. I used to explore the beaches up at Jenny Cliff mostly. I love the sea. It's so passionate and wild. Anyway, one day I saw Mr Tullen with his dog and I asked him if I could take his dog for a walk. He told me that the dog was quite vicious unless he knew people so I could take him on my own in the future but that it would be best if I went along with him today as he walked his dog, so the dog would get used to me. We went walking along the Hooe Lake and into the deserted quarry. I was quite happy, chatting about all the flowers we saw and was totally unaware of the danger I was in when Mr Tullen said he wanted to show me something down an old building entrance. Too late I realised we had walked down a dead end. Mr Tullen told the dog to stand guard and then turned to me. He told me if I screamed or tried to run away he would set the dog on me. I don't want to go into details, other than to say he didn't, you know, he didn't ... go the whole way. But what remains with me always are two things. First: the memory of feeling like I was going to die because I couldn't breathe when he put his mouth over mine and secondly: the knowledge that I'm sullied." I am quiet for a moment as I digest the fact that for the first time in my life I am trying to explain how I feel.

"I couldn't tell anyone, he told me he would tell everyone I was lying and that I was just a naughty girl and then when no one was looking he would set his dog on me. My days after that were filled with fear every time I went out. He found me playing with my dolls one day in the waste land near our house. He told me that when he put his finger inside me he knew I wasn't ready yet, as I was too small, but not too far away I would be ready for more than his finger." Now I stop. Feelings of loathing flood through me, I want to scream with the helplessness that I had felt. After a short while – when the silent screaming has stopped, three words are racing around inside my head, *I am steel.* When the inner voice finally stops I continue.

"Eventually, Mr Tullen was arrested for raping a young girl in the village. I was really sad for her and understand how afraid she must have been, and I felt so guilty I hadn't told anyone. But I was also glad when they sent him to prison because after that I never saw him again. My entire life I've spent looking down, not wanting to look up and meet the eyes of any strange man, and never wanting to draw attention to myself. I told myself I was dirty and worthless and I didn't deserve to meet a nice man. It's funny because up until that moment if anyone ever asked me what I wanted to do when I grew up I used to reply, I want to be married, have children and live in a cottage with roses growing on it. I thought I was asking for the simplest of things, little did I know I was asking for the near impossible." I pause again and listen to Bob's heart beat which has slowed down now. I am filled with gratitude as I realise he has just held me to make me feel safe and has listened without interrupting. *You're such a lovely man.*

"I don't know how to love you, Bob. I got married to George because I was pregnant not because I loved him, I don't regret it because I have two wonderful children, but I doubt I would have married him if I hadn't have been expecting. It would have been best if I hadn't married him because then we wouldn't have hurt each other. I want you to look for someone who can love you the way you deserve to be loved. I don't want to hurt someone else, I don't want to hurt you."

"Give me a chance Alix, let me love you, what have you got to lose?"

"You don't understand Bob. I was the class dunce at school, and well, going for a walk with Mr Tullen just emphasized how totally stupid I really am. The only way I could cope with the craziness inside me when this happened was to decide I was made of steel. I shut down my emotions; I locked them away inside a hardened heart. I told myself that no one would hurt me again. I've not really loved anyone, except my kids, since that time."

"Take a chance on me Alix."

I am quiet for a while. The irritating inner voice is yelling warnings at me, but I ignored it.

"Okay."

Chapter 11

September 2001

Alix and Suzi dating catch-up

"So what's new?" I ask. Suzi grins. We've met for a quick catch up in Starbucks.

"We are up to 'R' already, his name is Richard."

Suzi had been on Plenty of Fish and had discovered that there was certainly plenty of fish out there. However a lot of them needed throwing back into the sea pretty instantly. Men, and women, on web sites tend to lie rather a lot and so it had taken several disastrous dates to begin to know the warning signs and to implement safe guards.

"Well after the last date with Mr Little Liar I wasn't holding my breath on who would turn up." Mr Little Liar had been a man on Plenty of Fish who had put in his profile that he worked for the police force and gave the impression of being a hunk. Now Suzi is only five foot tall so when her date turned up and turned out to be smaller than herself she ended up having one of the quickest dates ever. Not that she didn't like small men, simply because she was fed up with the men she met who had lied, and so she told him outright that he wouldn't meet the woman of his dreams if he carried on lying.

"So I was pleasantly surprised, to say the least, when Richard met me in the car park of the pub. He isn't the most handsome of men but he is quite attractive and he was so easy to talk to it was great. In fact at the end of the date when he walked me to my car I nearly asked him to come home with me."

"You didn't?" I ask quickly. Suzi smiles at me.

"No, I could hear you telling me off in the back ground, it's not the third date – why did you shave your legs – why didn't you wear your Bridget Jones knickers – why didn't you wait until he invited you to his house? Your voice is quite persuasive you know!"

"Thank goodness for that," I sigh.

"I was a good girl, I waited until the third date and I waited until he invited me into his home, had a quick look around, no signs of a girlfriend."

"Better safe, than sorry. So far so good, though somehow although your jolly I can kinda feel a 'but' coming along."

"You know me too well. We'd been out for a lovely meal, which he paid for, and then we went back to his house for a night cap. We didn't get as far as the kitchen, he grabbed me in the hallway and started kissing me and that was that. He took me in the front room and got me to stand in the middle of the room whilst he sat on the settee. He told me he was going to tell me what to do and I was to obey him."

I give a little shake of my head and smile, I had no idea at all how many men out there are into kink of some description. I can honestly say that when it comes to sex I had led a remarkably sheltered life, up until my forties that is.

"Richard told me to undress in front of him. Never had that before and it was thrilling, but you know I think I prefer being the one in charge, love to whip a man! I do like being told what to do, but really I prefer being dominant. But no matter how much I suggested I tie him up he wasn't having it, oh but it was good."

"How do you always manage to find men into kink?"

"Well, it might have something to do with my Fish profile" Suzi winks.

"Why what have you put?"

"I change it often, but at the moment it reads along the lines of, 'If you're not too tied up why don't you come out to play?' Things like that." I start laughing.

"Never! You didn't really write that did you?"

"Sure did, and when I wrote, 'Let's have some really whipping good fun', you should have seen the hundreds of emails I got." Both of us laugh and I shake my head at Suzi.

"You're being careful aren't you?" I ask. Suzi frowns slightly and takes a drink of her tea.

"Oh Suzi, don't tell me you're not being careful."

"It's just so hard when you get a man who knows what he wants, and you know what a turn on that is, well how do you say no to him? And really I've never met a man yet who likes wearing them."

"That's not the point."

"I know and I promise to be safe going forward." Suzi lets out a sigh.

"Anyway that's not the end of it, he's a man apparently who really only likes sex when it is in a threesome, so now what am I to do?"

"Did he ask you for a threesome?"

"Yep, says he has female and male friends who would pop along for some fun."

"Damn, but where do all these people come from? What are you going to do?" I ask.

"Nothing, it's not for me threesomes, nor is taking coke so I've called it a day. I actually feel ready to take a break. I don't think any woman in the world has been on as many first dates as me. It's exhausting. Plus if you have too many 'forth dates' it actually gets very expensive as well. I practically live in Anne Summers and I've had to buy a new cupboard for all my sexy underwear!"

"You're happy though?"

"Yes, actually I feel pretty good. The kids seem to have settled down in school and college, work is going well and I've actually been able to cut down my dose of Prozac. I have one guy I'm speaking to at the moment called Jake, he's a real hunk so I've got my fingers crossed, however, if he turns out not to be right I'm seriously giving up this dating lark. How are things with you at the moment?"

"Good, like you I've dropped the dosage of Prozac which I'm over the moon about. I've decided to give Bob another chance, he's so nice."

"Are you sure you're doing the right thing?"

"No, I'm not, I have this sickening feeling that I will hurt him and I really don't want to."

"That's not a good enough reason to stay with someone, Alix."

"I know. Work's going well too by the way, made some nice friends there and I'm beginning to clear off my debt which is such a relief."

"You just changed the subject."

"I know."

Chapter 12

Sat 29th September 2001

Suzi and the dedicated libertine

Although Suzi really enjoys sex she is put off by men who sex-text. It makes her feel cheap and does nothing to turn her on, so the men who start that after the first date normally never get a second. It was one of her no-no's.

However, her stomach spins a bit as she reads Jake's text. Oh, but he's clever. His text reads – Suzi don't be late, I am impatient to have you in my arms. I can't wait to smell your hair and hear your voice. Oh and ps get inside your knickers! His confidence fills her with desire and she can't wait to get to his house. She sends a quick text back – Who says I'm wearing any knickers?

She's about to start the car when Jake texts back – Get here now! She turns the radio on to Key 103 and pulls the car off the drive smiling. It's a long drive to Chester but Suzi doesn't mind. Jake has driven all the way to Cheadle twice now to take her out for a meal and she is happy to go to his. She'd been to Chester loads of times, as she loved the old walled city, so she was quite confident she would find his house using his instructions quite easily.

His house is a four-bed detached new build on the outskirts of the city and must have cost a pretty penny. She spots his Jag on the drive as soon as she pulls into the cul-de-sac and she pulls her Focus onto the pavement outside. The front door opens instantly and there he is. Jake's five foot seven inches tall and quite slim, but he works out and is all muscles. With black hair and blue eyes he really is striking. She turns the engine off but before she can open the door he is there opening it for her. He gives her his hand and helps her out of the car before shutting the door and then instantly pins her against the car whilst he pulls her head to his and starts kissing her.

Suzi is taken by surprise, *what will his neighbours think?* After a moment he pulls himself away from her reluctantly.

"Bag in the boot?" he asks. She nods, she has no breath left to answer him. He gets her bag out and takes her car keys off her to lock it. She follows him into his house where he puts the bag on the floor and then reaches behind her to shut the front door.

They crash into the wall as Jake grabs her and starts kissing her fervently.

"Hi," Suzi says, when he finally stops snogging her and comes up for air.

"Hi," he replies huskily, as his teeth nip her neck. Then his hand is moving up her legs and she feels desire flood through her. Up his hand goes, to where her knickers should have been. Jake moans as his fingers find no obstruction to her private part. "You naughty girl." Suzi's body is alive, every part of her tingling. Jake manoeuvres her to the stair case and sits her down. He starts undoing the buttons on her dress with his teeth whilst his hands move over her body. When her dress falls back he stands up, pulls his top off and undoes his trousers, kicking them away. He stands there completely naked and hard, his eyes bloodshot with lust. Suzi reaches up and traces her finger over the dragon tattoo that he has running over his stomach which ends at the beginning of his pride. He moans in pleasure as her wandering finger runs down the dragon and then along his erect manhood. He pulls Suzi up and turns her around to kneel on the stairs and then he guides himself inside her. She moans in pleasure as he fills her. Then, despite his hunger and his urge to have her, Jake moves slowly. Going in and out at different angles building her pleasure until Suzi is moaning loudly. As her insides contract and pulse, she lets out several small moans. He needn't wait any longer and now he starts thrusting with all his power in and out until at last he flushes her with his come.

****

Just then a car cruises very slowly past the house.

"That's her car, this must be the house, pull over, love." Suzi's dad pulls the car over and stops but doesn't turn the engine off. Chris looks at his wife and sighs.

"I don't think she'll be pleased with us if we knock on the door."

"Oh, I'm sure she won't mind. We'll just explain that we're in the area visiting your uncle and just happened to see her car."

"She'll think we're spying on her."

"Don't be daft she'll be fine, we'll just go in for a quick cuppa and check everything's okay."

"She's thirty-three for goodness sake Anne, she'd as much like to see us right now as she would dance in a pit of snakes." Chris pulls the car out and starts driving away.

"I just want to know she's safe that's all."

"I know love, I know."

****

"That's funny," says Suzi pulling her dress back on.

"What is?" asks Jake.

"Well, I caught a glimpse of a car going past the window just then and it looked just like my parents car."

"Really?" asked Jake, "do they live around here?"

125

"No, they live in Cheadle near me."

"That's okay then, probably not them. Fancy some dinner now?"

"Be lovely, I'm starving all of a sudden," Suzi answers with a laugh. Jake takes her hand and leads her into the kitchen. The table is set for two, complete with gothic candle holders and flowers. Suzi takes in the Cesar salad, fish platter and the fresh baked rolls and is impressed, it was simply quite perfect. Jake does an elaborate bow and indicates she should sit.

They eat leisurely washing down the food with two bottles of Bordeaux whilst asking each other numerous questions that reveal the person behind the date.

"Last question. Favourite film?" Jake asks.

"Easy, Family Man with Nicolas Cage." Suzi answers.

"Why?"

"Because it's about what matters in the world, love and making the right choices, no matter how many times I watch it I end up crying. Choosing family over money is the honourable thing to do even though it means giving up his silver Ferrari! And yours?"

"Star Wars. I just *love* the fights with the light-sabers." Suzi bursts out laughing.

"Come on," Jake says. "Time for bed." Suzi looks at her watch, she had arrived at seven and it was now ten, she hadn't realised so much time had passed, still it was early.

"You're tired?" she asks.

"Hell no, it's time to get kinky."

"Oh."

Kink for Jake, turns out to be watching group sex on TV, whilst having sex with Suzi in every position imaginable. By the end of the night she is quite surprised to discover how versatile and bendable she is. She is also completely shagged out and exhausted and more than a little relieved when he finally falls asleep.

The next morning he brings her up some breakfast in bed, after she's drunk about half a cup of tea he starts covering her naked body in bits of the fruit salad so he could lick them off her with his tongue.

At eleven o'clock she starts getting ready to go home, as she has a quick shower she wonders on whether Jake is the one for her. He's handsome and charming and a great lover but would she like to introduce him to her kids? She comes out of the bathroom wrapped in a big white towel to find Jake sniffing a line of coke. Well that answered that question. No, he wouldn't be meeting her kids.

Chapter 13

20 March 2004

The Girls

Sleep-over's are not just for kids. Going out is fun, getting dressed up, plastering the makeup on, all part of life, chatting up strangers in the pub – all good fun. But the nights I enjoy the most are girlie sleep-over's. Pj's, Bacardi, nibbles, sometimes a rom-com, but always, always a night filled with laughter and putting the world to rights. I turn up with a cooked chicken and a full bottle of Bacardi, my contribution to our night in. As usual I am the first to arrive, after bear hugs in the hall I go straight upstairs to get my 'comfies' on. By the time I get back downstairs, Suzi has poured two large Bacardi and cokes and emptied a bag of crisps into a bowl.

"Cheers!" we chime, clunking our glasses together.

"Come on then, tell me all about it, how did the date go?" I ask.

"Which date?" answered Suzi with a chuckle.

"How many dates have you been on?"

"This week?"

I laugh, "Yes this week."

"Let me see, there was the teacher in that nice little Italian in Cheadle on Monday evening, the lawyer in the coffee shop on Tuesday lunch time and then the farmer last night in the pub."

"I thought you were giving up on men for a bit?"

"I did, for three whole months. It was awful! Felt like I was slipping into a convent, simply had to do something about it quick, you know what they say, 'use it or lose it'." She's being flippant; we both know how much she longs for that one special person who will complete her. Just then there is a knock on the door followed by a "Hello, where are you all?" That announces Polly has arrived.

"In the kitchen" yells back Suzi.

"Great stuff, will leave the door open, Sophie's just pulling up." Not long after we're all sat around the kitchen table in our pyjamas.

"Cheers," said Sophie. "Cheers," we echo as we clash our glasses together.

"Right, who's starting us off?" asks Polly.

"I think Suzi should," I say, "she was just about to give feedback on this week's dates."

"Dates?" says Sophie, "how many have you been on?"

"Only three," Suzi protests.

"Well, how did they go, anyone a keeper?" asks Sophie. I sit back in my chair slightly and watch my three friends talking about men. Polly is beautiful, tall and slim with long brown hair and deep blue eyes. She is always so elegantly dressed, and style is a natural flair for her. To look at her appearance you would think she shopped in the most elite of shops, but she doesn't, she just has a knack of picking up bits and throwing them together to give off the air of relaxed sophistication. Sophie's another stunner, with gorgeous locks of naturally curly, blond hair, a little freckled nose and laughing blue eyes. Suzi is as tiny as a Barbie doll with soft auburn hair and a china doll look of delicacy about her. I feel like an ugly duckling next to them. With bottled-blond, shoulder length hair, a little nose, and a small mouth I consider myself a very 'plain Jane'. The only thing I know I have going for me is my ample bosom, and I only have that due to being overweight.

"Actually none of them were keepers," Suzi answers, "no spark at all with any of them, to be fair I think they felt the same."

"How many dates have you been on now?" asked Polly.

"Too many that's for sure but I think I've got the handle on it now. I know what I'm looking for, thanks to Alix and her insistence on making a list," Suzi pauses for a second and raises her glass at me.

"What kind of list did you make? Not tall, dark and handsome I hope?" chips in Sophie.

"No, a real list," I answer.

"Things like, does he like family life; is he just as happy staying in and watching telly as much as going out and does he likes dogs? Things like that," answers Suzi. "I wanted to add to the list 'does he like giving head,' but Alix wouldn't let me." Sophie splutters her drink and mops it up quickly with a tissue whilst trying not to choke.

"I thought you might have a whole list for sexual preferences," says Polly giving Sophie a hefty slap on the back and passing another napkin to her.

"She wanted to," I retort, "but I made her pick ten things that had nothing to do with either looks or sex. After all girls, as we know, looks are skin deep and don't mean anything and sex is fleeting. So, if we're looking for that long lasting relationship then we need friendship to be on the top of any list."

"I agreed with her," Suzi nods, "but when Alix wasn't looking I wrote another list with the top ten 'must do it bed' list."

"Oh great," says Polly, "let's have it then, mine would have to include foot massage."

"What, in bed?" I ask.

"Oh yes, I'd lie back on the bed and do my breathing exercises and my partner would massage my feet at the same time. First it completely relaxes me, and secondly it turns me on."

"But not everyone likes feet," I say.

"I know, and that's how I know I found the man for me when he actually enjoys doing something to me that I love."

"I would have to have a man who enjoys reading in bed," says Sophie.

"*Really?*" asks Suzi. I get the giggles.

"Yes, sex is great fun but I love curling up with a book before I go to sleep so I need to be with someone who enjoys the same thing."

"I once drove bloody miles for a date only to be told, although I seemed like a very nice person, as I didn't go jogging, I wasn't the one for him," I say, "so you see even men have their lists."

"So what is on your sex list?" asks Sophie.

"Not sure I'm drunk enough yet," answers Suzi.

"Oh go on," I urge, "we all know what you're like anyway."

"Well size is on my list. That saying that goes 'size doesn't matter' is a myth created to protect men's egos. Size does matter, especially after you've had kids."

"I agree," I say. "I once heard that having sex after kids is like throwing a banana down the high street." Everyone giggles except Polly. She's reached forty-three and still not met her Mr Right-for-her, so the chances of her having kids one day are getting very slim.

"That's why it's important to do your pelvic floor exercises girl, keep it nice and tight," says Sophie pulling in her tummy as she speaks to demonstration how easy it is.

"I do mine in the car," I add, "that way I'm doing them at least twice a day."

"I've bought these egg things that you put in, you have to grip them to keep them in, they say it tightens you up really good so I'm giving them a go," says Suzi.

"Blimey, you can buy just about anything these days," I say shaking my head, "anyway what's next on your list?"

"Kissing," answers Suzi, "love being kissed deeply."

"Oh, me to," chips in Sophie, "could spend forever kissing deeply and passionately."

A lengthy discussion about what makes a good kiss follows between them, I sit quietly, sipping my drink.

"You're quiet Alix," says Sophie after a while.

"Kissing's not my thing," I answer.

"Why's that?" asks Polly surprised.

I shrug, "I don't know really," I lie. "I just don't like it, makes me feel a bit like I'm suffocated. George once told me that he thought our marriage didn't work because I wouldn't kiss him and be intimate with him. He could be right I know, but somehow it just felt like he was blaming me for the fact that he slept around."

"Men are very good at that," says Sophie.

"I remember one time I made George a cup of tea and put it on the coffee table next to him, he nudged the table and knocked the tea over and then had a go at me telling me it was my fault because I put the side-table too close to him. Everything was always my fault." I look down at the table for a moment, reliving for just a second, the anger I had felt towards George. *I am steel.* I lift my head and smile, "anyway that was a long time ago, back to this list Suzi."

"Doesn't Bob mind that you don't kiss?" asks Sophie.

"Yes he does, but I do kiss him, he makes me, in a very nice way."

"How?" asks Suzi.

"He just tells me to kiss him, in such a way that I know it really means a lot to him for me to kiss him. So I do. It's the first time in my life I have French-kissed anyone."

"So do you still feel like you're suffocating then?" asks Polly.

"Yes," I answer without hesitation. "I can only kiss him for really short periods and then I try and distract him by saying I want to kiss him all over."

"I couldn't imagine not liking kissing," says Sophie, "I feel that it is the part of a relationship that is so intimate it glues you together."

"I like kissing too, so long as it isn't a wet slobbery kiss, really hate those," says Suzi.

A very humorous hour follows with a sharing of sexual preferences, all washed down with a fair bit of alcohol.

"Shall we eat now?" asks Suzi standing up. "Before we end up legless due to lack of nourishment?" Everyone agrees and like a pre-planned military operation we start emptying tubs, bags and packets until a 'help your-self' feast is on the table. I'm slicing the loaf, Sophie's washing cherry tomatoes and Polly's putting the kettle on, for much needed cups of tea. Suzi's holding a carving knife in her hand and looking at the cooked chicken on the plate.

"This is the boniest chicken I've *ever* seen in my life," she moans. I look over at the chicken and burst out laughing. I stand up next to Suzi chuckling away, then lift the chicken up with two forks and turn it over.

"It's not so bad," I say, "when you have it the right way up."

Chapter 14

Sep 2002

Alix – You can't force love

We'd taken a week's holiday off as soon as school time had started again. Neither of us liked the bustle of streets packed with people. So one gorgeous sunny September afternoon we drove up to the prettiest little cottage you had ever seen, in the middle of nowhere, just outside of the village of Presteigne in South Wales.

The cottage was picturesque black and white and surrounded by a tree-filled hill. Bob had picked it for very specific reasons.

We unpacked our stuff as quickly as possible and then took off, hand in hand, to explore the surrounding countryside. Not far away a ruined fort stood on a hill. Ignoring the warning sign to stay out as unsafe, we went in to explore. The two of us were fascinated by old things and my imagination ran wild as I imagined who had lived there. It was soon dark and we returned to the cottage to have cold chicken and salad washed down with Rosé wine.

When we had cleared up Bob told me to go upstairs and put a skirt and top on. I practically ran upstairs, I loved our games.

Back downstairs again Bob was waiting for me in the front room. The curtains were drawn and the log fire crackled away merrily. He stood tall with his hands behind his back.

"Come and stand in front of me." I did as I was told whilst grinning up at him.

"You trust me?"

"Yes, of course I do." This statement was always a perpetual puzzle for me. I trusted no one in day to day life, and relied only on myself. I was the only person I knew wouldn't let me down. So why when it came to sexual role play did I trust Bob? I still haven't worked that one out.

He pulls his hands from behind his back and covers my eyes with a black silk mask that he ties tightly around my head. I'm excited; I never know what he's going to do but I do know he will delight in pleasing me. Next, he pulls my hands behind my back, clasping steel handcuffs around my wrists. Then he places a leather collar around my neck, locking it with a small padlock.

I hear him rummaging about and wonder what he's doing. His hands are suddenly at my neck taking hold of the metal loop that hangs at the front of my collar. I realise he has put something through the loop when suddenly my neck jerks upwards. Although I can't see what he's doing I can hear and sense him and I realise he's tying me to the large metal ring that hangs from the middle rafter.

When he's finished I am basically 'hung'. My toes curl in the carpet fibres whilst I fight down thoughts that I might be in trouble.

Bob holds the back of my head gently whilst he slowly pours a little wine into my mouth. I hadn't realised it was coming and some wine spills over the edges of my mouth and runs down my neck. I hear him put the glass down then he's back, licking and kissing at the spilt wine. He kisses the top of my breasts through the thin, see-through blouse I'm wearing. My nipples, clearly on display as I don't have a bra on, are now standing to attention and Bob moves his mouth down to suck one then the other through my blouse. I am very quietly whimpering in pleasure.

His hand slides under my skirt, reaches up and pulls my panties down.

"Step out of them," he commands, "but be careful to keep your balance. If you fall you're going to hurt your neck."

Standing with a rope attached to my neck collar, and with my hands behind my back, I realise standing on one leg is going to be slightly more nerve wracking than it should have been. I hear Bob sit on a chair to watch me. My undies are down around my ankles so it shouldn't be too difficult. I slowly lift one foot and instantly feel myself wobble so put it down again. I bite my lower lip concentrating on keeping my balance, and then try again. I do it quickly this time, lifting my right foot out of my panties and down again before I have a chance to wobble. Now feeling confident I flick the garment away with the left foot. I hear the chair creak as Bob stands up. I'm shocked when I hear and feel him rip my blouse off.

"That cost me twenty-five pounds what are you doing?" I yell. Bob whispers in my ear.

"I'll buy you another one. Now, no more talking." I'm not a hundred per cent sure I'm happy about my blouse being ripped but my mind is brought back to the moment when something suddenly stings my breast.

"Ouch," I mutter.

"Did that hurt?"

"Am I allowed to talk now then?"

"Yes."

"No, not really."

"Then why did you say ouch?"

"Not sure, just the shock I think."

Bob rummages through his bag and suddenly he's gagging me. Really this is too much – he'd asked me a question after all! Then the sting is back again and demanding my attention.

"If the wax becomes too much I want you to shake your head and then I will stop." *Wax? That's what's stinging me?* Bob carries on dripping the wax over my breasts until he's practically smothered them. Then he's taking photos from every angle, I can hear the 'click-click' of the shutter. I had been very weary of him taking photos of me at first but Bob had assured me they were for his eyes only and that they meant so much to him, so in the end I had consented, I trusted him. Camera down Bob comes back to me, unties the rope from my collar and removes the gag.

"Kneel." I obey and slowly drop to my knees. "Do you want a drink?" I nod, I'm not going to talk and risk the chance of being gagged again. I sip at the glass Bob holds against my lips. Once I'm done Bob places the glass back on the table and then I hear him undress. I imagine his tall, muscular body and his firm chunky thighs and my excitement grows. Oh, I so want to feel him inside me.

He places his hand on the back of my head and pulls me forward slowly until my lips meet his swollen member. I eagerly take him in my mouth, well half of him; he's too big for me to manage any more. I play, sucking hard then soft, flicking my tongue over the tip of him until he is moaning in pleasure. After only a couple of minutes, he stops me and withdraws.

"I don't want to come yet." He bends down behind me and removes the handcuffs. I'm glad because having my hands behind my back for too long hurts, and I shake my shoulders to release the muscles. Then Bob's hands are around me, cupping my breasts and gently squeezing, cracking the candle wax which falls in bits all over the floor. He kisses the back of my neck, sucking hard until it hurts. My inner walls convulse in pleasure. *Fuck me, oh please fuck me.*

He lays me down on the carpet and starts kissing the front of my neck whilst his hand draws hastily up my thigh and plunges inside me. I moan, arching my back.

Suddenly he's laying down and swinging me around at the same time so I end up on top of him. His right hand reaches up and grabs the hair at the back of my head so that he has me in a tight grip. I pull myself up so that I can straddle him. I want to see his face but he hasn't removed my mask so I'm in the dark and have to imagine the pleasure that might be there. I take hold of his hard member and slowly lower myself down. I am careful and go slowly because actually, Bob is too big for me, and although I like bondage, I'm not *really* into pain!

Slowly, I raise myself up and down again. I can't see Bob but I can hear him, his breath becomes louder as he nears his peak. Then suddenly he's moaning, his hips trembling as he fills me.

A few minutes later, we're in the shower together. Bob takes a hot, soapy sponge and tenderly washes my entire body. He is big and strong but his touch so gentle and loving.

If I can't love this man then there must be something wrong with me. I remember something my mum once told me, that people can talk themselves in and then out of love. I had thought it quite true, but now I knew differently, because no matter how great the sex is, or how wonderful a person Bob is, I just wasn't in love with him, and no amount of talking to myself was going to change that.

That night when we lay naked and locked together in a perfect hug, I feel safe and loved, and so very sad. *If only I could love him.* As Bob falls asleep, my mind races over the things we had just done. How is it possible, after an experience in my childhood that turned me off loving and trusting men due to a man overpowering me, did being dominated now turn me on so much? It was a conundrum, which maybe only years of counselling would reveal the answer. However, I am steel and self-sufficient, no counsellor for me.

The next few days were full with lovely, slow paced, sightseeing trips and numerous breaks for coffee. The best afternoon tea ever was at Ludlow castle, hot strong cafetiere with huge, light and fluffy scones with generous portions of clotted cream and jam. Not only were the scones great but sitting outside on the paved area looking across at the castle was my kind of heaven. My Nan had filled my head with stories of fairies and magic and my step Dad and taken me to visit many castles in Wales. My imagination is still full of magic and romance of times gone by. Ludlow castle is beautiful, we hold hands as we walk along the high parapets and observe the lovely scenery below the castle. I feel like a child and I'm filled with a spirit of adventure. The great thing about a holiday during the week when everyone else is at work, is the fact that places of interest are practically empty. The sun pours down on us and my dress blows upwards several times in the strong wind. We are laughing as we enter a turret and start climbing the narrow spiral staircase. At the top I kneel on the cold stone and peer through the arrow slit, I'm just about to turn to Bob to say he should take a look when suddenly he's kneeling behind me. I half turn to look at him and whisper, "Really?"

He ignores me; lifts my dress then pushes my undies to the side and enters me, all before I have time to object. After the initial shock, I feel a thrill go through me. This is *so* naughty; anyone might decide to come into the turret at any moment. Bob is obviously really excited, because the thrusting doesn't last long before he's stifling a muffled cry and coming inside me. I shake my head at the craziness of it. Bob looks so quiet and shy, you'd never believe how experimental he is.

On the last day when we're driving home I'm filled with mixed emotions. I consider myself an honest person, not someone who plays with people in any shape or form. I feel that I do love Bob, who wouldn't? He's such a lovely person, but I know I'm not *in* love with him, and so much of me yearns for that movie-style type of crazy love, the one that sweeps you off your feet and leaves you breathless. The kind of love I believe is only possible in the movies and is a far cry from the reality of life, and yet, the kind of love I long for. I wasn't being fair to Bob by staying with him, he deserves to be loved by someone like that, and I know that will never be me. I have to tell him we're finished, I have to. Yet, panic, fear and dread lurk within. Raising their Medusa-style grip on me, confirming what I know is true. I am a wicked person. I will always be on my own. I will die old and lonely. And most importantly, I don't deserve to be loved.

Chapter 15

October 2007

Alix and Suzi do the Lakes

'I will Survive' is playing on the radio. I scrunch up my face in protest and look out of the window. *Oh, how I hate this song.* Suzi is singing along to every word blasting her lungs for all her worth. When it's finished, I look at Suzi who is driving the four by four and ask.

"Club anthems, please?" Suzi laughs. It's Friday and four o'clock on we are driving up to the Lakes for the weekend. Neither of us have kids at home this weekend and both of us are looking forward to simply relaxing.

"Tell me again why you're not interested in this guy?" I ask.

"You mean Tom?"

"Yes, he sounds to me like he's perfect for you, I don't understand why you won't give him a chance."

"Well he has a girlfriend for one" replies Suzi.

"I know, but you told me he said that was really over and they were sleeping in separate rooms and that they're only together until they sell the pub."

"He's not free and I'm not interested."

"Yet you've accepted his invitation to come and spend the weekend in his pub?"

"Well, I'm not adverse to a free holiday! And besides Anne will be there so he won't try anything on. Plus I am quoting him for some advertising for the pub so this is really a business trip and not a free-be holiday."

"If you say so. Any dates recently?"

"I'm still on a break" Suzi answers. "Been six months now, you know? I'm going to concentrate on building up my business, keeping the kids happy and looking after my body. I've even joined a gym."

"Have you?" I answer quite surprised. Suzi has always declared she didn't have time to run to the shops let alone run on a treadmill.

"Yes, I feel all empowered by the new me! I actually feel happy," she gives me a quick smile before turning her head back to looking at the road.

"I'm so pleased for you. You deserve to be happy so much. So you're giving up on men for the minute then?"

"Yes, I've got lots to keep me busy. My business is really taking off, you sure you don't want to come and work for me?" I laugh.

"No thanks, we'd never get any work done!"

"Yes, probably true."

Two hours and fifteen minutes of driving and chatting and we finally pull up in front of the pub near Lake Windermere. The Pig and Pheasant is a gorgeous old pub, stone built with a thatched roof, totally picturesque and utterly rural. The walk from the car to the pub turns out to amuse both of us. Heels have no business walking over cobbles and mud. We have come for two nights, which might have surprised any on-lookers as we emptied the boot of several large bags and literally stagger across the cobbles with them. By the time we reach the entrance we're helplessly giggling.

We ask the barmaid if Tom is about, and within minutes he is bounding towards us, his pleasure at seeing Suzi written all over his face.

"Your room is back outside," he said.

"Really?" we both answer at the same time, knowing instantly the heels and cobbles are about to encounter again. Tom takes Suzi's bags off her and I look at his back as he marches off, slightly put out. Suzi grabs a bag off me and we hurry after him. He stops at the bottom of some very steep metal steps, more like a ladder really.

"It's up here." We both looked at Tom in shock and burst out laughing. We really aren't dressed for metal ladders, both in dainty shoes and miniskirts.

"Lead the way," Suzi says, nodding at him when he steps back to let us go first. He bounds up the stairs two at a time while we hold tightly to the bannister and follow very warily. Tom shows us quickly around the mini apartment, one bedroom with a double bed, small sitting room, shower room and kitchenette.

"I'll see you at dinner then," he says before leaving.

"No drinking for us tonight then," I muse to Suzi, looking at the steep steps.

As the sun is already setting, there's no time to go exploring so we decide to unpack and get dressed for dinner. We both throw our suitcases on the bed and start putting stuff on the sides. Suddenly I catch a glimpse of Suzi's suitcase and burst out laughing again. Six pairs of the highest heels are laid in a row in the case.

"We've only come for two nights," I laugh.

"I know, but I want to be covered for every outfit I brought along. You never know who you're going to bump into – you told me that. Always wear makeup and make an effort because today may be the day you meet 'Mr Perfect for you'."

"I know but *six* pairs of heels?" Then a thought strikes me. "You did bring your walking boots didn't you?" Suzi pulls a face and shrugs.

"I didn't think we'd need them?"

"We're on a walking weekend!"

"I thought the only walking we'd be doing would be between the Swan and the Bull's Head."

"We're supposed to be ambling, not pub crawling." Suzi fishes in her bag a moment and then pops up holding a bottle.

"I brought Bacardi," she says with a grin.

"Then all is forgiven," I laugh. We go to the kitchen to find glasses and pour two large drinks of Bacardi and coke. "So, what are you wearing this evening?" I ask.

"I'll show you." We go back to the room and Suzi pulls out of her bag the most gorgeous cocktail dress.

"You don't think that maybe that's a *tad* too much for here?"

"I'm dressing for myself not for anyone else. This dress makes me feel as sexy as hell and I like that feeling."

"It's not for Tom's benefit then?"

"No, it's not. How many times do I have to say, I'm not interested in him."

"Okay, then I best dress-up myself." When we're ready I look at the steps.

"Maybe we should wear wellies?"

"And ruin the image, I don't think so. Come on Fluffy, let's go get them farmers!" We giggle down the steps, across the cobbles, into the pub and all the way to our table in the restaurant. The only people standing at the bar are indeed local farmers, who all wear sensible wellies. Not too sure if it was having a weekend of freedom, or too much Bacardi but we laughed all the way through dinner. After the main course Suzi took herself off to the loo, and while she was there a party of people arrive and go to the bar. *Posh lot from the city.* They probably have all the good rooms, which is why Suzi and I are out in the old barn, still our rooms are free, so I'm not complaining at all.

As Suzi came out of the toilet she notice the group at the bar straight away, she gives them a quick smile before weaving her way through the tables back to me.

"Do you know them?" I ask her.

"No, why?"

"Well, that gorgeous hunk there can't stop staring at you."

"Who?" said Suzi, swinging around in her chair to take a look. She scans the group for a brief moment and then she finds the man I'm referring to.

"I do know him, but I'm not sure where from." Suddenly the 'drop-dead' handsome-hunk is making his way towards us and Suzi's face flushes bright red.

"Hi," says Mr Drop-Dead Hansome.

"Hi," we both say back.

"I think I know you but I'm really sorry I can't remember where from," Suzi says.

"Excuse me, could you tell me where the business awards are being held?" For just a moment Suzi's face is blank and then she twigs.

"The Mere Hotel!"

"Yes, and again in Cheadle, when apparently, I saved your Christmas."

"Saved dinner, but not Christmas, I'm afraid." The stranger looks at her questioningly.

"I'm Suzi," she says sticking her hand out, "and this is Alix."

"I'm Jonathon," he replies, shaking first Suzi's hand and then mine.

"Are you here all weekend?" he asks.

"Till Sunday morning," Suzi answers.

"I've got to go now because it's my brother's party, but could we go for a coffee tomorrow do you think?" Before Suzi has a chance to decline I chirp in.

"She'd love to, meet you here in the pub say eleven?" Jonathon turns and smiles at me.

"That would be perfect." Jonathon gives Suzi, a big grin that make his eyes sparkle, then returns to his party.

"What did you say that for?" Suzi hisses at me. "He's divine but I'm not dating at the moment, remember?"

"Well it's not a date really, just a cup of coffee. What's the harm? Now tell me all about the other times you met him."

The next morning we have a quick bowl of cereal and then go our separate ways. Suzi goes for a business meeting with Tom and Anne, whilst I pull on my walking boots and head for the lanes.

It's a lovely day, the sun is shining and birds are tweeting from every direction. Contentment floods through me - I love the countryside. Within a short walk down the lane, I find a footpath heading off through the fields. I haven't gone far when I realise it is too hot for my thin jumper and pull it off and tie it around my waist. Short sleeved t-shirt cooling me down. I always feel like an adventurer when I embark down a path I've not gone on before, I'm constantly on the lookout for that old ruin or that twisted tree that Fairies live in. *We might have to grow up in the world, but in our heads it is quite acceptable to stay as young as we like.*

I miss Bob, and I know he would have loved this walk. *I hope he's happy and that he's met someone really nice.* For a few minutes I let my mind wonder on the things we did, not just the sex, which was great, but all the day trips and exploring we did together. I sigh as I recall the email he sent me after I finished with him for the second time, after coming back from Wales. It was angry and hateful and I didn't blame him at all, I deserved it. One bit of the email though had cut me hard. 'I went out with you even though you're fat.' Ouch, below the belt, so very, very below the belt. But he was right, no one would ever love me the way I dreamt of being loved. I was too plain, too fat and way too boring. Just for a moment I feel the tears well up behind my eyes and give my head a good shaking.

I don't need a man in my life to be happy, and I'm certainly not going to cry about it anymore. I look at my watch, ten to eleven; I've been walking for two hours now, time to turn back. I wonder how Suzi will enjoy her coffee with Jonathon. He's so handsome, I wouldn't mind if he smiled at me the same way he'd smiled at Suzi.

11 am

Suzi strode into the bar half expecting Jonathon not to be there. He is, leaning against the bar, watching her as she walks over. He's dressed in his casuals today, and Suzi notes he's just as handsome in jeans as he was in his suit. She looks him over as she approaches; he's too handsome for her and way too tall. He stands up straight as she reaches him.

"I thought we'd take a ride into Keswick if that's okay with you?" Suzi hesitates for a moment; she thought this was a quick coffee in the lounge?

"I need to let you know that I am not dating at the moment," she said, looking him straight in the eye.

"That's fine because I'm not asking you on a date." He scrutinizes her face.

"Just coffee and a stroll through Keswick?" Who could resist his smile?

"Well seeing as you asked so nicely how can I refuse. I'll just go and get my coat and put a bit of makeup on."

"It's lovely out you won't need a coat and you don't need to put any makeup on." She raises a lofty eyebrow at him.

"The sun's shining and we're not going on a date remember?" Just for a moment, Suzi is struck by the thought that she doesn't know if she finds him irritating or extremely attractive.

She wasn't impressed with his flashy BMW either. Her ex had driven one whilst speeding them along into bankruptcy. She was turned off by money-men; she didn't believe them to be real people with their feet on the ground. She never, ever wanted to open the door to a bailiff again – one of the reasons she pushed herself so hard in her own company. And behind an Armani suit, and a car that cost way too much, lurked the suspicion that once it was gone the man would disappear too.

"You're judging me," Jonathon said, as they sat at a table near the most beautiful stream that trickled merrily through the restaurant's garden.

"No I'm not, don't presume to know me!"

"You don't like my car, you've clocked my shoes and my watch and nothing impresses you. So I have to conclude, you're judging me."

"We're on a 'none-date' for a cup of coffee, why would I judge you?"

"I don't know, why don't you tell me?" They look at each other in silence for a moment.

"I'll start," says Jonathon. "The first time I saw you, I wanted you." She can't help it, she smiles. "Obviously being mistaken for the waiter wasn't very flattering but you were flustered so I forgave you, whilst thinking I would give almost anything to take you to bed."

"Hey, I'm not that kind of girl!"

"I know you're not, another reason why I am so attracted to you. I couldn't get you out of my head. I wished nearly every day that I had at least asked your name. After a time I told myself to get a grip and forget you. I ended up getting divorced the following year." Suzi tried to keep her face in neutral but she felt a skip inside her when she realised he was now single.

"And then you were there again, getting out of your car and going into the curry house."

"You saw me before I slipped?"

"Yes. I had been about to drive off when you pulled up in front of me. I watched you looking out of the restaurant window and I felt like a teenager that didn't know what to do. I decided I would go and talk to you and ask if you wanted to meet up with me, but I couldn't bring myself to do it in-case you rejected me. Then when you came out and you slipped..."

"...And you caught me."

"Yes, but as I did so I realised that you had a wedding ring on and that you had obviously got dinner for a family, your eyes were sparkling too and you looked so happy. So I walked away."

"I wasn't happy for much longer that day."

Suzi and Jonathon end up spending hours together that day and they never once, stopped talking. By the time he drove them back to the hotel she was smitten.

Chapter 16

09 February 2007

Alix and Suzi do the Trafford Centre

I look down at my mobile then smiling quickly type back a message to Suzi. Yes I am free for tea and yes 6pm at the Trafford Centre is fine. It's been a while since we last got together for a catch up. I have got used to the fact that when Suzi has a man in her life she tends to disappear for a while. I don't mind, I know the silence means that Suzi is currently doing okay.

We meet in our usual place by Pizza Express. Both of us grin at each other as we bear hug before going into the restaurant.

"We know what we want thanks," Suzi tells the waitress as we sit down, "two diet cokes, a vegetable pizza and side salads, many thanks."

"We come here a lot," I say smiling up at the waitress. As soon as the waitress has left I sit back in my chair.

"And?" I ask with a smile. Suzi grins.

"I have so much to tell you I don't know where to begin!"

"Tell me about your dinner date then." Suzi sighs.

"It was perfect. He came to pick me up and we drove to the restaurant. When the waiter showed us to our table Jonathon said, 'No this won't do at all I want to sit back there, where it's intimate'."

A very big sigh flows from me.

The waitress turns up with our cokes and Suzi stops to smile at her, waiting until she leaves before carrying on.

"He's so dominant, yet a complete gentleman and he makes me feel so special."

"Lucky lady. How many times have you met up now?"

"Well, he had to go away for Christmas, so we've really been meeting up mostly since he got back in January, I would say we meet at least three times a week."

"Wow, that's good going."

"I think he's going to propose!"

"What?"

"I know! I know it's too soon but he was showing me pictures on his phone and he got to one and got all flustered and tried to flick past it quickly but it looked like a diamond ring to me."

"Okay, so you don't know for sure he's going to propose?"

"No, but he's asked me to go on a cruise with him in May, and thinking, wouldn't that be a romantic place to do it?"

'Don't build your hopes up, Suzi, after all you've only known w months."

"I know but it just feels perfect, like it's meant to be." I'm worried; Suzi has taken years to heal and has really only just got to that place where she is independent and happy to be on her own.

"Don't worry. Both my feet are firmly on the ground I promise you, well that's unless Jonathon has got them tied up somewhere." I laugh, which is what Suzi wanted.

"So tell me about you. You've been on your own for ages now Alix, are you going to go back on Match?"

"No, but I have joined a very naughty group, called Tagged. I'm chatting to a couple of guys on there. One called Gary and one called Pete."

"Tell me more."

"Gary seems like a lovely person, he's not divorced yet but separated, he's in the army and rides a motor bike and he is just a great person to talk to. He's had a rough time lately and I really feel for him."

"Umm, and the other one?"

"He's called Pete. Don't know much about him really, bit of a me-laddo I think."

"Well, he sounds interesting!" Suzi chuckles.

"I know but I really like Gary, we talk for hours and I think I'm falling for him."

"But you've not met him yet?"

159

"No, but that doesn't mean anything. You know which guys are on line just for fun and Gary isn't like that, he's a real gentleman and he's had such a hard time of it with his wife I feel really sorry for him."

"He could just be a player?"

"No, I'm sure he's not. He's never been suggestive or rude and we've just talked like best friends, I really like him." Suzi looks at me that look that means she knows what men are like and she doesn't want me to get hurt.

"And you're sure he's separated?"

"Yes. He's living in army barracks at the moment and calls me from there so I know he's not at home any more. Besides he spends ages telling me how much he misses his son, so I know it's true."

"Are you going to meet up then?"

I go slightly red. "Yes, we've booked a hotel for the weekend in the Lakes, I can't wait I'm so excited."

"Separate rooms?" Now I go really red.

"Well no, but Gary's told me he will sleep on the sofa bed and I needn't worry if I don't want to sleep with him." I look at Suzi a bit defensively, "crikey Suzi, I'm a grown woman I know what am doing." Women can say so much with just a look, and Suzi's look right now said ... *I'm not so sure.*

"And what has happened to the 'fourth date' rule?" Suzi asks.

"Well I feel like we've chatted on Tagged and on the phone for months now and it's like we've been on loads of dates."

"And the, 'no sex before you get into his house,' rule?"

"Well that's not possible is it, as he's living in barracks right now."

"You're breaking all your own rules," Suzi says with a frown.

"I'll be fine. I promise I'll be careful."

"Okay, just call or text me to let me know you're safe."

"Will do."

Chapter 17

Alix and the desperately seeking attention guy

After nearly eight months of messaging each other the weekend in the Lakes had finally come. I arrive at the hotel early, on Easter Friday the 6th of April. I want a long hot bath and plenty of time to relax before Gary arrives.

The hotel was tiny, really only a few rooms over a restaurant, set in a picturesque village alongside a stream. The old black and white timber building was a lovely, romantic setting for a first meeting.

I put a cd on the portable player I'd brought with me, poured myself a stiff drink and then sank into the hot bubble-filled bath. I had laid my corset on the bed and the clothes I would wear that evening. Outwardly: demure, quiet, middle-aged woman. Underneath: pure sex goddess waiting to be released. My mobile rings, I pick it up and look to see whose calling, some mobile number shows on my screen so it's not someone I know. I switch it off, I don't fancy talking to anyone right now.

Two hours later I'm sitting in the bar ordering myself a drink. A text comes from Gary to say he's arrived in the room and will be downstairs shortly. My stomach lurches, would I like him as much face to face as I did when we were talking? *I hope so.*

As soon as he enters the bar I feel the excitement flip inside me. He's dressed in a suit and obviously gone to a lot of effort. He hands me a single red rose and bends down to kiss my cheek before sitting down next to me. After just a moment of awkward chit chat we break into normal dialogue, throwing questions at each other in quick succession. Half way through his second pint of beer he suddenly goes quiet and looks at me.

"Alix, I have something to tell you. I wanted to tell you days ago but I just couldn't because I wanted to meet you so much and I knew if I told you that you wouldn't come." My heart sinks. *He's a player after all.*

When I don't answer he carries on.

"Two weeks ago my wife came to visit me in the barracks and persuaded me to go home. We're going to go to counselling together and going to give it another go." He looks at me waiting for an answer but my mouth is shut tight and I can't talk.

"I'm sorry Alix, I know I should have told you but I just couldn't, I was too selfish I just needed to meet you, even though it would just be this once."

"You'll have to book another room," I finally reply.

"There aren't any, I've already asked, they're full up. And I can't drive home now as I've been drinking. Let's have this weekend Alix." His voice softens, "Please? I will sleep on the sofa, I won't try anything I promise, I just want to have dinner with you and spend some time together, please?" I look down at the tablecloth for what feels like an eternity. *I don't know what to say to him, damn but I'm such a bloody idiot.*

Saved by the waitress. "Your table is ready, if you would like to follow me."
Not knowing what else to do or what to say I simply got up and followed the waitress, Gary did the same. The waitress asked if we wanted wine to which I replied, "No thanks, but I would like another Bacardi and coke." Left on our own the silence returned.

"Say something please." Gary reaches to take my hand and I withdraw it.

"You should have told me."

"I know. I'm sorry."

I look at him hard. Nice enough chap but only just a bit taller than me and I really do prefer taller men. I like the feeling of being small and needing protection. *If I had met him in a pub I probably wouldn't have fancied him.* But then all our long chats came back to me and I knew he was a nice guy. I believed him, I didn't think for a moment he had planned this all so elaborately just to get me into bed.

"Where does she think you are now?"

"Visiting a friend."

"You've only just got back to together won't she be suspicious of you going away so soon?"

"Honestly no. She knows I've always been head over heels in love with her, she is the one who has gone off in the past and found other blokes and I've always waited for her to come back to me. She doesn't think I have it in me to have an affair."

"We're not going to have an affair," I snap.

"No, no I didn't mean that, I just mean she doesn't question me if I say I am going to my brothers or my friends, she just says have a nice time."

"Are you ready to order?" a waiter asks. I look at Gary.

"I don't actually feel hungry."

"No, nor do I," answers Gary.

"Sorry," I said looking up at the waiter, "we'll just go back to the bar, if that's okay?"

We sit by an open wood fire in big comfy seats and drink whilst we try and talk about normal things. Work, cars, kids, money, politics, everything except the matter at hand, and what a bloody shitty world it is some times.

That night Gary slept in the double with me but we did no more than cuddle. I had already shut down, cold and hard like steel. I knew he was a gentleman because he told me he was back with his wife straight away and not whilst he was driving his motor bike off the next morning.

I left the hotel and drove slowly away. I was in no rush. The kids had left home and were doing their own thing and the house was empty. Tears spill out of the corner of my eyes and soak my face. Mingled emotions of self-pity and anger fight for dominance inside me. *Fucking men!* My mobile rings and I ignore it; I don't feel like talking to anyone. *I don't bloody get it, why can't they be happy with just one woman?* Twenty minutes later my mobile rings again. Curious now, to know whose after me I pull the car over into a lay-by and pick up the phone. It's the same number that called yesterday, intrigued I call the number back.

"Hello," I say quietly, not sure who to expect.

"Hi Alix. How you doing?" I remain silent, *who is it?*

"It's Pete here." I'm still silent, *Pete? Pete who?*

"Pete from Tagged."

"Oh hi," suddenly I realise who he is.

"So what are you up to?" he asks. I look up at the beautiful country around me. "Just driving around in the countryside, at the moment."

"Do you fancy meeting up for a drink when you get back then?" It was the last thing I wanted. "Ugh no, sorry, don't think I will be back until late."

"Okay no problem, what about tomorrow? We could go for some lunch if you like?"

"I'm really sorry but this whole weekend is booked up already."

"That's fine, how about next Sat?" *How on earth can I come up with another excuse not to meet him?*

"Yes okay, I'm free then." *That gives me a week to cancel.*

We arrange to meet in Manchester centre at 2pm the following Saturday. After I put the phone down I burst into tears. *I just want to be on my own, life is so much simpler that way.*

Chapter 18

April 2007

Truly Madly Deeply

"Pull it tighter."

"You sure?" I ask.

"Yes as tight as it can go" Suzi says resting her hands on hips.

"Okay, but we don't want you passing out now."

"If I feel dizzy I shall swoon and Jonathon will catch me." I chuckle as I pull the cords on Suzi's basque as tight as I can.

"Wow!" I say when we've finished. The basque pulls in the waist so much giving Suzi the most perfect hour glass figure. "Jonathon's a lucky guy."

"I've really fallen for him Alix."

"I know, I just hope for you that he really is a good guy."

"I believe he is. Like this weekend for example, he's suggested that we should have a weekend away together before we go on a cruise. He picked the date he knew the kids were with their dad and he booked everything. He just makes me feel like a princess." I smile back at Suzi, she is glowing and happiness is radiating from her, I hope to God that Jonathon is a keeper.

"Well I'll get going then, what time is he picking you up?"

"In twenty minutes." We have a quick hug and I go, all fingers and toes crossed that Suzi has a lovely weekend.

Fifteen minutes later the front door bell rings and Suzi's heart tightens in her chest with excitement. She's ready, she picks up her weekend bag, pops her designer sunglasses on and opens the door. Her stomach lurches, Jonathon's smile sets all her nerves tingling. *I love this man* she thinks as he gives her a peck on the cheek and takes her bag off her. All the way to the hotel she remains fairly quiet, her mind is working ten to the dozen on the pros and cons of falling in love. A large part of her wants to run away and make sure she doesn't get hurt again but a bigger part wants to be in his arms.

Neither of them has mentioned the L word but Suzi is sure he loves her; why else would he be looking at diamond rings?

Jonathon checks them in and they head into the lift. A young couple with a child in the women's arms get in with them. Suzi tickles the little girls chin and has a brief chat with the parents. The young couple grin, with a sparkle in their eyes, as Suzi chats absentmindedly.

When they get out of the lift and are approaching their room Suzi said, "They both had funny grins didn't they?" As Jonathon slips the room key into the lock, he turns slightly to smile at her.

"That might have something to do with the fact that your bag is vibrating."

"What?" Suzi yelps in surprise, and swings her bag around. Sure enough, there is a sound of vibrating coming from her bag.

"It's not a rabbit," Suzi declares indignantly, as they enter the room, "It's my toothbrush, see." She dives into the bag to fish out the offending item, going red. Jonathon bursts out laughing.

"Now that's a shame," he says throwing Suzi onto the bed. In a flash he's removing her clothes.

"What about a drink?" Suzi asks.

"Yes in a minute, but first I want this." He clambers onto the bed and over the top of her and comes down to kiss. At first his lips are soft and gentle but soon he is parting her lips so that his tongue can find hers. Suzi moans.

Artfully Jonathon removes her dress.

"Wow!" he says, as he looks at her basque and stockings. He jumps up and gets his phone.

"What you doing?"

"Got to take a picture of you, you're sexy as hell." Suzi rolls onto her side and places her head on her hand and sucks in her cheeks to blow him a kiss as he snaps away. When he is finished taking the pictures he pours them both a drink of Champagne.

"To us," he says raising his glass.

"To us," Suzi answers. As soon as the glasses are down Jonathon sets about untying her basque and setting her body free so that he can start smothering her with kisses. *I love you* is on constant repeat in Suzi's mind. He kisses her stomach with a hundred little pecks and then works his way to Suzi's bust. Slowly he traces his tongue around, working slowly towards her very erect nipples. When he covers her nipples with his mouth and sucks hard Suzi groans and arches her back. She wants him inside her, she needs to connect with every part of him. Her hands move down to his jeans and she undoes the zip before slipping her hand inside and caressing his rock hard member. There's no rush, and a slow rhythmic intercourse begins as they touch and kiss each other's bodies, heightening their need for one other.

When at last they come, they lay with their arms wrapped tightly around each other; eyes closed relishing how much they had enjoyed the last hour.

"I have three words I want to say to you," Jonathon whispers into Suzi's hair. Suzi instantly wells up. "Truly, madly, deeply," he whispers into her neck. Tears start falling down Suzi's face and onto Jonathon's chest.

"What's wrong?" he asks, leaning up on his elbow to look down at her.

"I'm frightened to love again." Jonathon reaches up his hand and very gently holds the right side of Suzi's face.

"I'll never hurt you Suzi, I promise." For a moment he waits to see if she believes him then he lies down and pulls her tight against his chest. He knows she loves him and that she will tell him so when she's ready.

Chapter 19

14 April 2007

Alix and the dream-date

"What do you mean you're not going?" demands Suzi down the phone.

"I just don't want to go, I'm going to send him·a text in a minute and make up some last minute disaster that's preventing me from going out."

"Don't you dare! Have you had a shower?"

"No."

"Get in the shower now Alix, I will be with you in ten minutes."

"I can't go Suzi, I've been crying all morning my face is red and puffy."

"Well, don't cry anymore and the shower will freshen you up, now get to it I'm on my way."

Half an hour later, I am showered, dressed and drying my hair.

"You can't go like that," said Suzi.

"Good, then I'll stay at home." Suzi was rummaging through my wardrobe and pulls out a yellow dress.

"How about this one? Very pretty and feminine."

"If I have to go then I am going like this," I reply gesturing at my pale jeans and soft pink tea-shirt that I'm wearing. "Besides I'm supposed to be there in half an hour, never going to make it in time so I might as well just call and cancel." As I reach for my mobile on the dresser, Suzi snatches it.

"No you don't, I'm going to text him and tell him you're running late but you're going." Suzi's fingers tapped quickly on the keys and then she put the phone down.

"Now then make up."

"I'm not sure make up is a good idea it will run everywhere."

"You're not crying any more, do you hear me?" Just then the mobile rings. I look at it in horror when Pete's name appears on the screen. Suzi picks it up quick, swipes the answer call button and holds it out for me to take. I give my worst scowl possible towards Suzi, then answer Pete's hello.

"Hi."

"So you're running late then?"

"Yes, sorry about that."

"No problem," Pete says, and I can hear him smiling, "you at the hairdressers then, getting all dolled up?"

"No I'm not," I answer flatly. "I'll just come as myself if you don't mind."

"Okay. Just wanted to let you know I'm here already, don't rush and see you when you get here."

"Okay thanks." I put the phone down and look at Suzi, a few tears are rolling down my cheeks. "I don't want to go."

"Well I'm driving you to Manchester, so you're going." Suzi sits on the bed and puts her arm around me. "Look, I'll drop you off and then go shopping somewhere. I'll stay around for about an hour and if you don't want to stay with him just text me and I'll come back and pick you up. Okay?" I nod.

"Thanks."

Forty minutes later we're nearing the pub in Manchester. I'm still dabbing at my eyes, ever so gently, to mop up the occasional tear. I feel so unattractive right now. We pull up outside the pub and I look at Suzi to see if there is any chance she would change her mind.

"I won't go home until you text me that you're alright." I give Suzi a smile of thanks and get out of the car. I watch the car pull away and then turn to the door just as it opens and Pete comes out.

"You made it then," he says with a smile. *Blimey, but he's handsome. His photos don't do him justice at all.*

"Yes finally, sorry I'm late."

"Never mind, come on in. I've got a table by the window. What would you like to drink?" No hesitation.

"Bacardi and coke please."

I sit at the table that Pete has pointed to and wait for him to get the drinks. I watch him at the bar laughing with the barmaid, *damn but he's hot.* He must be about six foot two inches, trim firm body. Great dress sense in well worn-in designer jeans and one of those tops that say, 'I don't have to wear a shirt to look smart'. Soft light brown leather loafers finishing off the air of, 'I know I'm getting on but I still do trendy'.

He brings the drinks to the table and smiles at me, his brown eyes sparkling with mischief. *God, but he's a confident chap.*

"Cheers," he says, clinking his pint glass against my tumbler. Pete starts plying me with questions, making me talk and taking my mind off everything except for this date. After a while he stops talking and looks at me.

"You're not yourself today are you?" *No. He's perceptive, as well as handsome?*

"Not really. Sorry."

"It's okay. We're just having a drink and getting to know each other. Nothing to worry about, I'm not an axe murderer or a sex offender." I open my eyes wide at him and he laughs, a rich warm laugh from deep inside. "Seriously, I'm a good guy, well most of the time. Why don't you tell your friend she can go home now?" I burst out laughing. I look at his lined craggy face and his short salt and pepper hair and suddenly, just like that, I'm smitten. If you'd asked me previously whether I believed in love at first sight I would have laughed and replied, of course not. And although this wasn't technically first sight, it was within twenty minutes of meeting him and I can't believe the strength of feelings that are flooding me now. Love, at first sight? Lust, at first sight? Whatever it was it filled me with electricity and made me feel more alive than I'd ever felt in my life before.

After a further ten minutes of listening to Pete talk, and laughing at his ribbing I knew I could let Suzi go home.

"I'm just popping to the loo." I say, standing up.

"You mean you're going to text your friend. Tell her 'hi' from me." I go chuckling all the way to the ladies-room where I quickly text Suzi, to say all is ok and I'm staying. I look in the mirror. *Oh shit.* My mascara has run and I have a thick black smudge under my left eye. Quickly, I get some tissue and wipe at it as gently as possible not to make my swollen eyes any worse. I apply some lipstick and gave my hair a quick brush. I might not have minded what I looked like when I arrived but I certainly do now. My cheeks are rosy; nothing I can do about that, it's the downside to drinking alcohol. But my eyes are sparkling. *Best of a bad job, just hope he's had enough to drink not to notice.*

When we finish our drinks Pete asks.

"So where do you want to go now?"

"I don't know," I say shrugging my shoulders, "I don't know Manchester."

"Really?"

"Yes, really."

"Okay, let's go on a pub-crawl then."

"A pub-crawl. *Really?*" Pete laughs at me.

"Come on," he says, grabbing my hand.

Oh my God, he's sooo handsome! We dash into a couple of pubs, down a drink and rush off to the next one. Eventually we turn up at the tiniest pub I have ever seen. Mr Thomas' Chop House, a Victorian piece of history. Its terracotta brickwork framed in black iron, a massive coat of arms over the entrance and underneath a plaque declaring 'Est 1867'. Towering over the pub are modern buildings and I love the fact that something so beautiful has survived the trials of time.

It is packed and we have to squeeze our way to the bar. A pint and a Bacardi later and we spot a table in the corner and squeeze our way over to it.

"Not lager this time?" I ask, looking at Pete's dark pint.

"No. Whenever I come here I drink a pint of bitter to remember a friend of mine."

"Who was that?"

"Just someone who meant a lot to me." We're quiet for a moment and then Pete turns to me with a glint in his eye.

"So where were we?" I laugh. Pete has been trying for the last hour to persuade me to go home with him.

"I've told you, I don't *go home* until at least the forth date."

"What are you doing tomorrow?"

"Nothing, why?"

"There's a market I like going to, I just wondered if you would like to come with me?"

"Yes okay, what time?" Pete writes his address on a beer mat and hands it to me.

"Is nine thirty too early?" I grin, I am an early bird.

"No, that's fine."

We leave Mr Thomas' hand in hand as Pete leads us to the next pub. We walk some distance through the streets of Manchester and then turn into quite a small road, more like a back alley, called Half Moon Street. Nice name, I think, for not such a nice street.

"We're here," said Pete, and I look up at him in surprise, was he kidding? There were no pubs in this street. Pete grinned down at me. "Come on," he said. He went up to what looked like the back entrance to a restaurant, a couple of beer kegs were on the pavement next to a modest door. A black sign on either side of the door declared 'Corbiers Wine Bar' and I wonder where on earth Pete is taking me.

As we make our way down the narrow winding stairs the Happy Mondays 'Halleluja' comes rushing up to greet us. My eyes open wide as we enter the subterranean cave that is Corbiers. *What a fab place.* Pete heads to the bar and I do a quick dash into the loos. Normally I hated looking at myself in the mirror, hated the fact that I am so plain and far too chubby. But now all I can see are my sparkling hazel eyes. I feel alive. A quick touch up of lipstick and then back to find the man who was making my knees weak. I search around the plain square wooden tables until my eyes fall on him. He is grinning at me in amusement and my insides lurch as our eyes lock on each other. *Oh God I'm in trouble.*

"Don't sit there," Pete said, as I go to sit in the chair opposite him, "sit here," he said tapping the chair next to him. I slide into the chair next to him and he pulls the chair up so our legs are touching. Shivers of excitement run up my spine as he places his hand on my leg.

"On Thursday," he said, "I'm meeting some golf mates for a quick drink, do you want to come?"

"Yes," I answer, far too quickly. *I would probably say yes to anything right now.*

"Good, I'll pick you up at seven."

"You don't know where I live."

"You can tell me tomorrow when you come to mine." I get the feeling he's secretly laughing at me.

"Now," he said, "where were we?" I burst out laughing.

"I'm not coming home with you."

"Why not?" Pete asks whilst he slowly inches his hand down my back and inside my jeans. My insides are going nuts. I want, more than anything, to rip off all his clothes and jump on him.

"I can't go home with you, I have my Bridget Jones knickers on," I answer very seriously.

"*What*?" he laughs.

"I don't have sexy underwear on," I whisper.

"Who gives a fuck?" I reach for a drink to buy some time.

"I do." *After all we only get one chance to make a first impression!* I take another drink. *I will crash diet, damn, I won't eat a thing – well no chocolate, lettuce leaves and carrots here I come.*

We stay for a while in the cool atmosphere of Corbiers, listening to the juke box, sometimes talking, but mostly kissing. *Kissing.* If someone had asked me I wouldn't be able to describe what was going on in my head let alone my body. For the first time in my life I didn't feel like I was suffocating. I enjoyed the touch of his full, soft lips on my mouth, enjoyed beyond explanation the feeling of his tongue exploring my mouth. Not only did I enjoy kissing him back but I didn't want to stop. I was so lost in his kiss that it took a moment or two to realise his hand had slid under my t-shirt and was cupping my bust. I pull back and knock his hand away, furtively looking around the room to see if anyone has noticed. One bloke sat at a table on his own is grinning at me, so I know he had seen. Pete grabs hold of my wrist and I turn my head around to look at him.

"Don't ever knock my hand away." *Oh crap.* I understand that most women would be appalled at being told what to do but I loved it. How he knew I would love it I had no idea. I couldn't answer, just sat looking into his eyes that seemed to be sucking my soul into his.

"I have to go before I miss the last train," I finally say.

"Don't go home. Let's get the tram and go back to mine."

"No." I have no idea where the strength to say no to him comes from. All I want is to be naked and in his arms. But men aren't to be trusted. All very well having a one night stand with him if that was all I wanted, but every fibre in my body knew I wanted more.

He walks me up to Piccadilly train station.

"You're like a little kid aren't you?" Pete says, looking down at me. I grin, being described as little, in any form, is a lovely feeling. To be honest if I had known he was so tall I probably would have worn heels instead of my white pumps. He came onto the platform with me, despite my urges that he could leave once we reached the station.

"Not a safe place here at night," he said. We stand snogging with fervour, both our bodies crying out their need to be sated. I'm breathless when Pete finally pulls away.

"I wasn't expecting this," he whispers.

"Expecting what?"

"Go on, quick get on the train before you miss it."

I stand in the train door way and smile at Pete, I'm so happy.

"Next Friday I want to take you to this lovely Italian place I know. It is cosy and the tables are discreetly placed. They do great food. Would you like to come?"

"I love Italian food!" I answer.

"Good, that's a date then. Now text me when you get home so I know you're home safe."

"Okay will do," warm feelings of being looked after wash over me.

"Oh and Alix."

"Yes."

"Friday will be our forth date, so make sure you wear stocking and suspenders and leave those bloody Bridget Jones knickers at home." I burst out laughing just as the train doors shut.

When I get home I am still on a high and my brain is in one-to-one conversation in major overload. *OMG I've met this guy and just had the best date of my life. I liked kissing him! No, I loved kissing him. For the first time in my life I didn't feel like I was suffocating, I felt alive. He's so good looking and oh, so sexy. I'm filled with excitement and dread at the same time. He's going to find me boring I know it. He's so smart and sophisticated and I can hardly open my mouth to talk, I'm not going to be interesting enough for him I'm sure. Oh but please Lord, let him like me because without a shadow of a doubt I've met my other half.*

Chapter 20

Alix and the disappointing-date

I jump out of bed the next morning. I'd fallen asleep re-living every moment of the best date of my life. I'm so excited about seeing him again and nervous at the same time, would he still want to kiss me without his beer-goggles on? I take my time in the shower, shaving and re-shaving my legs to make sure they are silky smooth. *Not that he will find out how smooth they are, just I will feel more sexy knowing how smooth they are!*

Market – what on earth do you wear to a market when you are on your second date? I decide on a short denim skirt and a button up shirt, white pumps again, heels would have to wait until the dinner date. My stomach crunches again, how had he known I would own stockings and suspenders? I take extra care drying my hair so it lies in a straight bob and try my best to do my make up so that I look my best without the appearance of wearing too much. I only ever put make up on when I am going out so I'm no expert, still a bit of eye shadow, mascara and plum coloured lipstick and I have to admit I probably look the best I can.

I study the way to his house on the map and get in the car. I feel so nervous and my hands are trembling. *No big deal, we're just going to a market.* By the time I pull up outside his house I feel sick. What if he'd been joking and he wasn't really going to the market, I had checked my phone a hundred times but he had not texted this morning to ask if I was coming, or to cancel.

I go to the door and gently knock on it. *I don't even know if this is his real address.*

The door opens and there he was. Tall, handsome and slightly distant.

"Come in," he says opening the door wide for me. I'm nervous now, had I made a mistake coming? As soon as the door is shut he spins me around and pins me against the hallway wall, then his mouth is on mine and the feeling that something is wrong disappears. His hands are everywhere, holding my head, then on my back pulling me as close to his body as he can. Then they're on my breasts and on my legs. I'm on a rollercoaster and can't get off.

Every part of my body is trembling and I can't think straight. All I know is that I want him. He pulls me into the front room and somehow he has my shirt off before I know what's happening. He kisses my neck, *oh fuck,* and then works his way down to my breasts, kissing my ample bosom that's on display, being kindly assisted by my balcony bra. I want to explore and kiss his body but Pete's too busy kissing and touching me, like a boy in a sweet shop, greedy to taste every part of me. His pupils are dilated and fill his eyes, the rest of the white is covered in tiny red veins as lust consumes him. No talking, no seeking permission, just a need to fulfil the craving that surges through him.

He grabs my hand and puts it on his crotch and I can feel the size of him is massive. *Bloody hell, that won't fit in me.* Then Pete's undressing and in a flash, after removing only his top and jeans, he stands there naked, his member standing to attention. He spins me around and pushes me towards the settee. I automatically kneel on the sofa so he can take me from behind.

His arm snake around my body and pull me back against him. His fingers find my opening and he dives in to explore. I'm soaked already. He pulls back his hand and uses it to direct himself into me. I can't help moaning. His hunger, his need for me is all consuming. I have no thoughts, no doubts. I yearn to feel him inside me. He pushes slowly, his breathing getting heavy. My chin trembles in excitement and I feel the inner-walls start to contract. Pete moans out load and thrusts himself deeper into me. I yelp as the sudden thrust hurts and Pete withdraws slightly. Slowly he pushes into me, in and out, in and out, until my moans are those of wanton pleasure. Then he can't hold it anymore and his thrusts became deeper and quicker. I literally scream in pleasure as he finally releases himself deep inside me.

Then as quick as it had begun the passion is gone.

"Not too sure what the neighbours will think of that," he said pulling his trousers on.

"Where's the bathroom?" I ask picking up my clothes.

"Top of the stairs." I make a hasty retreat to gather my wits. I wash and dress and stand still for a moment. *What on earth have I done?* I come down the stairs slowly, not sure what to expect. Pete meets me at the bottom of the stairs, dressed and car keys in hand.

"Shall we go then?" he asks. I nod, I don't trust myself to speak.

We get into a fabulous old sports car and Pete presses play for some music. For a while we drive in silence. Then Pete asks me.

"You okay?" I didn't feel okay, I felt all at sorts.

"Yes ta," I said, giving him a smile to re-enforce the lie.

"Good. I thought you might be upset because it wasn't the forth date." I always take people at their word, never believe they are lying unless it's proven, and hardly recognise sarcasm when it comes my way.

"Actually, I'm quite flattered that you still wanted to have sex with me in the cold light of day, minus the beer goggles." I answer truthfully. *Well if I never see him again it's my fault for breaking my own rules.* The walk around the market was odd and I have no idea why we are here. Neither of us buys anything, and we hardly speak. I try once to take his hand – after all, we'd been holding hands last night, but he snatches it away. *Not a tactile person then, just as well I'll probably never see him again because I need a man who wants to hold me after sex as well as before.*

Back at his house Pete offers me a coffee but I decline. He gives me the briefest peck on the cheek before I get back into my own car. As I drive home I feel the cold seeping back into my body. *I am steel.* I feel flat and oh so bloody disappointed.

May

There's just no explaining love.

"I'm beginning to wish I'd never driven you to Manchester," says Suzi, pulling my basque strings with all her might.

"I'm glad you did, I have never felt so alive in all my life."

"He's a player Alix. We're supposed to run a mile from players, remember?"

"I can't explain it Suzi, I've never loved a man before and I didn't know it would feel like this. If he doesn't text me I feel like I can't breathe waiting for him to call, petrified I won't see him again. I know I should run a mile, I know who he is. But every fibre of me needs him." Suzi looks at me with sadness in her eyes.

"I hate him," she says softly. My chin wobbles.

"I know."

"I wish you could meet someone else, but I kind of understand. I'll always be here for you." We hold each other tight for a moment then go back to getting me ready.

" Did you manage to pick up some stockings for me?"

"Yes I did. I went to Wilmslow for you, here you go," says Suzi, passing me something out of her bag.

"Thirty five pounds! Are you crazy?" Suzi laughs.

"Just put them on."

I pull the stockings out of the box and let out a soft 'oh' for they're beautiful. So silky and sheen with little strings crossed over a line up the back of the leg and the top of them beautiful lace, very burlesque. I slip my legs into them and clasp them to the basque clips before slipping my feet into beautiful high heels. I wobble just a bit when I stand as I'm not used to high heels and take a look in the mirror. I hate my body and grab my long overcoat and put it on quick.

"He's not worth the effort."

I look at Suzi sad that I'm not able to explain to her that this man makes me feel beautiful, sexy and desired. I love him. Every part of me loves every part of him.

"He needs looking after so much, I just want to take care of him. It's so frustrating because I know I would make him happy if he would give us a chance. I'm hoping he'll realise he loves me one day."

"Maybe, but he has decided to use you and cheat on his girlfriend instead."

"Well technically he met me first so, really, he's cheating on me."

"Don't be stupid. He's a lying, cheating scum bag and I just don't understand why you're still seeing him when you know he has someone else." Ouch, sometimes we need friends to say it how it is, to keep our feet on the ground, to protect us from ourselves. After all, life is about choices and nothing else. Every choice we make has a repercussion – dick-head's decision had nearly destroyed Suzi, and I knew she didn't understand why I would cheat with someone who had another partner. She never said it but I felt that 'other woman' status over my head like the biggest condemning sign ever seen.

"You don't know him like I do, he's mixed up and depressed. He isn't really a bad guy."

"Yes, he is."

We hug tightly at the door as Suzi leaves, her way of telling me that although she doesn't agree with what I'm doing she still loves me. I pick up my overnight bag and double check everything is locked, then get in the car. A little shiver of excitement runs through me. If Pete knew I was coming to see him in a basque and coat he would be so excited. I drive to Pete's hoping that I won't be pulled over by the police. I seriously didn't want anyone else to know I'd come out without any clothes on.

I arrive safely, thank goodness, and knock on Pete's door with a smile. He opens the door instantly. After he closes it he made a move to grab me straight away, but I push him off.

"Take my coat off," I tell him. He looks at me slightly quizzed but does as I ask and removes my coat.

"Fuck!" he hisses, dropping my coat to the floor and pushing me up against the wall. He takes me on the stairs, on the sofa and on the kitchen floor and eventually, thankfully, we end up on his bed. We lie for a while, exhausted, and then Pete gets up.

"Just going for a bottle of red," he says pulling his boxers on. "What are you doing?" he asks whilst he watches me pull the blanket hastily over myself.

"Nothing," I answer pulling the cover up to my face. Pete looks completely puzzled and stands over the bed looking down at me.

"Why have you covered yourself up?" I can't lie and say I'm cold because it's a warm day and after the workout we'd just had we're both hot and sweaty. I just shake my head at him.

"Get up," Pete says pulling the blanket off me. Now it's my turn to be puzzled. When I'm standing next to him he turns me around and moving behind me, puts his hands on my shoulders and marches me over to the full size mirror.

"Look at yourself."

I try to turn away, I hate looking at myself. Pete turns me back to the mirror. I am bright red in the face, I'm so fat. This is awful.

"You are so fucking sexy, look, why on earth would you want to cover that up? You're God damn attractive, woman!" *I love you. I love you. I love you. It doesn't matter even if you're lying, I love that you want me to feel attractive. I love you.*

Chapter 21

Alix - Lust & confusion

I try very hard to ignore Pete's texts. Sometimes he has to text me three times before I answer! *Of course, I say that, tongue-in-cheek.* The trouble is, that even though I love Pete, knowing he has a girlfriend, *now, not a wife or fiancée or even someone who lives with him, just a girlfriend*, makes me feel shitty. I don't want to hurt another person and it doesn't matter that I tell myself if Pete wasn't cheating with me he would be cheating with someone else, *good gracious the rubbish that comes out of my head*, I know it's wrong. I call myself stupid at least twenty times a day; I berate myself for having no self-respect or will-power. I promise myself, over and over, that I'm never going to see him again.

Then he doesn't text me for two days and I'm holding my breath the entire time, because I will *simply die* if he doesn't want me in his life anymore. *Stupid, woman.* It's not like I can say I'm only a teenager, or I don't have much common sense, nope there is nothing wrong with me, except love. I need him. He fulfils me, completes me, and makes me whole. And I know, oh yes *I know*, he's the one, because he's the only man I have ever kissed passionately. The only man that sends an electric current racing across my skin whenever he touches me and the only man that makes me feel physically sick when I think I may never see him again.

This morning I got out of bed decided, enough is enough, I'm never going to see Pete again. That was several hours ago.

The first two times Pete rings I ignore my phone. When the phone rings for third time, my curiosity gets the better of me and I press the answer button.

"Hi."

"What you wearing?"

"What do you want, Pete?"

"To take you on a picnic."

"What?" He had me, I'm already smiling, *bloody hell but I'm so easy*.

"Pick you up in an hour."

"Where are we going and do you want me to bring anything?"

"It's a surprise, and nothing, I have it. So, see you in an hour then?"

"Okay." *I'm just going on a picnic, nothing needs to happen. Yeah right.* As soon as he hangs up I'm running upstairs for a quick shower and change. Before getting dressed I spray Very Irresistible all over my body. *Here's hoping the perfume describes my body, aye? Well one can live in hope. Not that we're going to have sex, just a picnic.*

Fifty five minutes later Pete is tooting his horn outside my house, I have a quick look in the hallway mirror and I'm relieved to see today is a 'good day'. Then I'm literally running to the car like a happy school kid.

"Did you invite Suzi to join us?" Just like that the joy of the moment is wiped away.

"No I didn't," I snap as I open the car door to get out. Pete puts his hand on my leg and I turn to frown at him.

"Good," he says, "I want you all to myself." And as quick as the anger had come it's washed away. I shut the door and put my seatbelt on.

As he pulls the car away I watch his hands, my stomach does a sudden lurch as I imagine them on my body.

"Maybe she can come with us next time?" Pete said with a smirk and before I can think of anything to say my hand swings out and I punch him in the side. He starts laughing.

I'm not sure where we drive to as I don't pay any attention to any of the roads the whole time we driving, but some time later Pete pulls into a deserted car park.

"There's a nice walk along the reservoir here." I look down at my sandals, not really walking shoes but at least I hadn't come in heels. Pete grabs a picnic hamper and blanket out of the boot then smiles at me. *Damn if you would only smile at me every day I would be the happiest person alive.*

We walk along for a while and then take a less worn path into the woods. I'm surprised that we walk for quite a while; I had no idea that Pete liked walking and I feel happy that we have another thing in common. Shortly we come to a beautiful clearing in the woods were the sun pours down and basks the grass in warmth.

Pete walks across the grass to the far side and lays the blanket down. I come to stand on the opposite side of the blanket and we look at each other.

"What are you most hungry for," Pete asks in a husky voice. I don't hesitate.

"You." He puts the picnic hamper down on the side and then kicks off his shoes. Without taking his eyes off mine he starts undoing his shirt buttons. I step out of my shoes and take my jeans off. Pete is taking his jeans off now as I pull my t-shirt off and drop it to the floor. For the entire time our eyes are locked together. He removes his boxers. I put my hands behind my back and unclasp my bra letting it drop to the floor. He stands opposite me, naked and hard already, his member proudly standing to attention. I slip my panties off, giving a quick look around the clearing, going slightly red at the thought that someone might just come walking by.

Pete stands on the blanket and I take a step onto it to stand in front of him. The sun is hot on my back but the breeze is cool and it drenches my body in its refreshing touch, making my nipples go hard.

Pete slowly snakes his arms around me and gently pulls me in, our naked bodies brushing softly against each other. His fingers curl around my neck as he holds my head and comes in for a kiss. Soft lips, inquiring tongue. My whole body is alive, tingling with the electricity that his touch always brings. My hands cup his gorgeous butt cheeks, I feel impatient. I already want him inside me. I pull his hips tight against mine.

Pete pulls back a little and smiles down at me, then reaches up and gently strokes my face before pulling me down onto the blanket with him.

We lay on our sides looking at each other. His eyes are red already and I know he is consumed with lust. The breeze has picked up and its cool flow washes over our bodies. I feel its touch on my thighs and between my legs. Over my breasts and down my back. Pete rolls me onto my back and starts kissing. My neck, my breasts, my stomach. His hands at the same time are moving up and down my legs. I arch my back. *Please fuck me.*

Then his hands are parting my legs. The breeze's cool touch races ahead of Pete's fingers and caress my soft lips, as Pete opens me the wind dives in. I'm moaning really loud, I can't help it. I'm beyond caring if anyone should come by. I just want him inside me, filling me, completing me, satisfying my need and my hunger. My hips are moving up and down. *Fuck me, fuck me.*

Then Pete shifts his position and I automatically open my legs to let him in. Just a second of positioning and then, oh God, at last. Pete pushes his hard member deep inside me. My shoulders lift me up and I throw my arms around him as he crashes into me, again and again. We stare into each other's eyes as lust consumes us. In and out, wave after wave. He devours me. His eyes demand my soul, and I give it to him willingly, and in return I draw his soul into my body. Pull it, draw it, like a magnet my soul clasps to his. My whole body is alive. My inner walls start contracting and I moan out loud, "Its coming". The convulsing is quickening and the wave starts. *Oh damn, oh shit, but I love this man.*

"Oh fuck! Wait for me babe." Pete must feel my building because his words are accompanied by an increase in the quickness and the hardness to which he slams himself in me. Then the shuddering release grips us both and Pete pushes himself so deep inside me it hurts. For a moment, he holds me extra tight as his body gives little shudders of release.

The breeze seems to have abated, withdrawn back, as inhaled ardour. Then a gentle gust releases across the opening and caresses our bodies, its touch intimate and seductive. Pete rolls over and lies down on his back panting. I look up at the sky, perfect light blue, interjected by a few white, fluffy clouds that are hurried along by the same wind that touches us. Perfect sky. Perfect day. If only I was with a perfect man, *no let me retract that, perfect people don't exist*, if only I was with the man who is 'perfect for me'. Dressed once more and lying on our backs I begin to regret coming with him. I'm so stupid. Because I love him so much, I believe that one day he'll realise that he loves me too. It can't just be about sex surely? The way he looks at me, pulling my soul into him. The way he touches me, as if every touch is something amazing. The way he is instantly hard the moment he sees me. It's got to be love, right? It can't just be about sex.

"Do you love her?"

"What!?"

"Do you love Lisa? It's a simple question."

Pete shuts his eyes. "But there's no simple answer." What I want to hear, is that it's me that he loves me and not her, but I can't ask that question because I'm afraid I already know the answer.

"You know I never told my wife that I loved her until the day she left me." I turn over and snuggled into his chest. "Why's that?" I ask.

"I just can't say the words. I think them but they don't come out of my mouth."

"Why did she leave?"

"Different reasons. I guess I am not a very loving kind of person and she needed more from me than I can give." *I can understand that.*

"She's a manic depressive and sometimes just can't cope with everything. One day I came home and she was standing in the hallway with her suitcases, she took one look at me picked up her bags and walked out on us. I thought she would get well and come back. She did get well but decided to start a new life with some spotty teenager."

"So she didn't leave because she found out you'd cheated on her?"

"What? No, I never cheated on her, she's my world." *Oh fuck.* All my insides were going nuts, he still loves his wife, he didn't love either Lisa or me.

"What happened after she left?"

"I had to give up my job to look after the kids, Keith needed loads of attention, he was the youngest and took his mother leaving really badly. Gerard and Hannah were no problem but I couldn't hold down my job as well as look after them. I had to sell the house to pay Amanda off and I've been in a slope to poverty ever since."

"Do you still see her?"

"Yes of course, she's the mother of my children, plus she calls when she's in trouble."

"And you race round on your white stallion to save her."

"I just help her out, that's all."

"You'll never love me."

"What? Where's that come from?"

"I don't need you enough, you don't have to come to my rescue or sort out any problems for me because I don't have any. I don't need rescuing."

"You're nuts."

"And you need to be needed. Come on, I want to go." Pete gets to his feet and helps me up then pulls me into his arms. My gorgeous, handsome giant.

"You know you're very special to me don't you?" I nod into his chest, I didn't want to talk anymore.

Chapter 22

October 2007

Suzi and the real guy

Suzi was so excited, in her heart of hearts she knew – well hoped, that Jonathon was going to propose to her on this holiday. Seven days sailing from Corfu then up the West coast of Italy was a dream come true in itself but to be with Jonathon and to have the hope he was going to propose, well she was practically high as a kite. Jonathon on the other hand, seemed slightly subdued and not quite himself and if she had asked him once then she'd asked a hundred times, are you feeling okay? To which he responded, yes just a bit tired. In the end she had decided to let it drop before she drove him crazy and he changed his mind about proposing.

She'd enjoyed the few hours they had in Corfu before boarding the ship but now they had unpacked she felt like their holiday had really begun. *Will he ask me tonight?*

She went into the bathroom to freshen up and check her makeup, after a couple of minutes Jonathon called to her.

"Babes come here a minute." She smiled in the mirror, *maybe it's now?* She came out of the bathroom trying to be all demure and composed but when she saw Jonathon she took one look at him and burst out laughing. He was completely naked – except for a black dinner bow tie - and standing in a bodybuilders bicep pose. Now although Jonathon was nicely trim and firm he was no bodybuilder and the fact that he was naked with a hard on tickled Suzi's funny bone and she got the giggles.

"Well you're not much good for a fellow's self-esteem, now are you?" says Jonathon before making a grab at Suzi and pulling her onto the bed. He tries kissing her on the mouth but she can't stop giggling so he moves onto her neck then down her décolletage. Suzi moans slightly and Jonathon moves back up to kiss her mouth again, only for Suzi's shoulders to start shaking as she fights to keep the laughter in.

"You're hopeless," he says, whacking her with a pillow. She instantly jumps up, grabs another pillow and hits him back.

"So," he laughs, "you want to play?" He brings his pillow high ready to knock her with it again but Suzi jumps off the bed, her pillow tightly held – ready for battle. Of course, it was an easy fight for Jonathon to win and after a few minutes, he has her pinned to the bed, the pair of them panting and laughing. Suddenly Jonathon is still as he looks down at the auburn haired beauty he had pinned beneath him.

"I love you," he says, staring into her eyes.

"I love you too," she answers. Jonathon stares down at her for a moment and then he is undressing her. Forty-five minutes later, they lie on the bed hot and exhausted.

"I can honestly say I've never met a woman who enjoys sex as much as you do," says Jonathon. It was her cue to build his ego.

"And I can honestly say I've never seen a naked body pose before," she answers. They burst out laughing and Jonathon pulls her into his chest and holds her tight.

"Nor have I ever been with a man who fulfils me so much." He nuzzles into her hair and kisses her forehead. They drink some champagne and chat away for a while before getting in the shower together. As Jonathon washes Suzi's hair, she feels his member rising and knocking against her back. She smiles and put her arms behind to grab him with soapy hands. As he washes the shampoo out of her hair, she starts rubbing her cupped hands up and down his proud manhood. Before long, he's groaning.

Jonathon spins Suzi around and pushes her against the shower wall then in one move picks her up by the bum and pins her to the wall. She grips his body with her legs and pulls him in close. His hand behind her neck pulls her face towards to him. As his tongue slips into her mouth, his hardness finds its own way inside her. The shower falls hot and fast and soaks them as they kiss and fuck with fervour.

"Bloody hell woman, you'll kill me off at this rate," pants Jonathon. Suzi laughs.

"That's not fair; it was your idea to save water and shower together." He bends down and nips her neck.

"Come on you hussy, let's get ready for dinner."

They both scrub up well, Jonathon in his immaculate dinner suit (bow tie included) and Suzi in a gorgeous body hugging silver dress. They walk into the restaurant arm in arm and Suzi, for once in her life, feels like a million dollars.

They're seated at a circular table for eight, and very quickly make acquaintances with the other people. There is an elderly Texan couple – who turn out to be hilarious, an elderly English couple – who are 'awfully' posh, and a younger French couple – who can't keep their hands off each other. The mix of personalities turns out to be lots of fun. The Texan's loud, good-humoured tales are tempered by, the 'plum-in-mouth' dryness of the older English couple. The French couple smile with chic detachment and loose themselves in each other's eyes.

The silver-service dinner is washed down with as much wine as they want. Needless to say, as the evening wears on the noise level in the room escalates and the louder it gets the more they needed to raise their voices to be heard.

"What did you say?" Suzi asks of the Texan wife.

"She said," replied her husband, "that when the air-con in the car didn't work, she still kept the window up."

"Is that to keep the dust out of the car?" Suzi asks.

"Hell no, darlin'," replies the Texan's wife. "It's so that no one would know we couldn't afford to fix it!"

"Wasn't that really hot?" Suzi quizzes.

"Yep sure was, sweat used to run down my back somethin' awful."

"I think I'd rather just open the window," Suzi replies.

"When I was a young gal, I used to draw a black line with a kohl pencil down the back of my leg so people would think I still owned a pair of stockings that weren't shredded to bits," said the older English lady.

"Mighty good fun trying to rip them off with your teeth, let me tell you!" laughed her husband.

"Willard!" snapped his wife, but the whole table was laughing enjoying the banter.

When the meal is finished the band comes on and the dancing begins. They change partners with their new found friends and dance until all the ladies heels are tucked under the table. When Suzi is dancing with the Texan he comes in a bit too close and Suzi goes straight into the Dirty Dancing scene of waving her hand in front of her stating, "This is my dance space." The Texan laughs and replies, "Sorry, always did have spaghetti arms, Baby." When they finish the dance and are walking back to the table he pinches her bum none too gently. It had been a really pleasant evening but Suzi was ready for some alone time.

"Do you fancy a stroll?" she asks Jonathon when she gets back to the table.

"I was just thinking the exact same thing," he answers standing up. 'Good nights' said, Jonathon takes hold of Suzi's hand as they walk out into the fresh air.

They wander in silence for quite a while and Suzi realises that Jonathon is looking for somewhere private for them to sit. *Maybe he's going to ask me now?* Eventually Jonathon picks a secluded bench near the swimming pool. The area is empty as there was no swimming allowed after 8pm. They sit on the bench and watch the Moon bounce its light off the swimming pool water. Jonathon's still holding her hand.

"What are your dreams Suzi?" he asked.

"Gosh that's a big question."

"I know, but what are you dreaming of, what do you really want in life?"

"I want my kids to be happy and well adjusted."

"Yes, I want that too. But what do you want for you?"

"I think I would quite like to go skydiving."

"I'm being serious."

"So am I. Imagine falling in the air it would be exhilarating."
Suzi looks at Jonathon's face and realises he's trying to be deep.

"I want what every woman wants, Jonathon. I want to grow old with a man I love, who loves me back in the same way."

"I don't think that is what every woman wants Suzi, I've met an awful lot of women in my life who are only looking for money. My first wife was like that but unfortunately I didn't realise just how much so until we had been married for a while."

"I'm not interested in money."

"I know, and it's one of the things I really love about you."

"Don't get me wrong, I like money. I like what money can buy, like lovely holidays, and especially security. There is nothing like being broke and not knowing how you're going to survive to make you appreciate that, of course, money is important. But it's not the *most* important thing. Being loved for who you are is the most important thing."

Jonathon squeezes Suzi's hand tight and takes a deep breath. *I do, I do.* Just then a pile of naked teenagers come charging across the forecourt and jump into the pool. After the initial shock of getting wet Jonathon and Suzi start laughing.

"Come on, let's go back to the cabin," Jonathon says pulling Suzi off the bench.

The next day was spent on board, ordering breakfast in the room and having a leisurely day swimming, sunbathing and reading.

A quiet comfortable ambience enveloped them all day and Suzi began to let go of the dream that Jonathon was going to propose.

The following day was the port call of Naples. Suzi was up as soon as the sun began to rise, she was so excited.

"Come on," she said, pulling the covers off the bed, "I want to be one of the first off the ship". They shower and dress whilst having coffee in the room then make a dash for the station where they will disembark to go ashore. Like kids, they hold hands and walk with a spring in their step as they make their way from the dock to the town centre.

They walk through the labyrinth of old streets enthralled by the beauty of the higgledy-piggledy, mishmash of colourful buildings before entering a small ristorante in a quiet cobbled alley. They order Sfogliatelle and Cappuccino's and practice their few words of Italian with the plump, cheerful waitress. After a few hours of walking round, they jump in a taxi and go to the Miranapoli Café. They're shown to a table outside on the terrazzo, and Suzi sucks in her breath at the beautiful sight of Mt Vesuvius in the distance, and the cascading town of Naples below them.

They wash their Neapolitan pizza down with a carafe of red Taurasi and linger for as long as possible, to absorb the wonderful atmosphere. After coffees and Cialdone Caprese ice-cream it's time to head back to port.

Later that night when they were snuggling into each other before dropping off to sleep Suzi muses over the lovely day and concludes that if Jonathon hadn't proposed at the extremely romantic spot in Naples then she had got it wrong, and he wasn't going to. She gave a little sigh, it didn't matter. She'd never been so happy.

The rest of the cruise was just as lovely as the first two days and Suzi was only slightly upset because the time seemed to be racing so quickly. Besides the day trip to Florence, when it had rained all day, the rest of the holiday had been lovely and sunny and surprisingly warm. And here they were on their last night aboard ship and Suzi wished they had another week exploring not only Italy but each other.

"Last stroll around the ship before bed?" Jonathon asks and she nods. They walk at a leisurely pace around the decks and eventually come to stand at the bow's edge. They lean against the railings watching the white horses on the waves below doing their eternal dance. Suddenly, Suzi notices Jonathon step back as he pulls something out of his trouser pocket and she looks at him in surprise.

"I'm not, what you might call, a mushy romantic type but I know that I fell in love with you the moment I saw you." Suzi looks at him, tears brimming over at the realisation that he's about to propose. Jonathon began to kneel.

Phhhhhhrt!

Suzi instantly giggles then throws her hands over her mouth to stifle them.

"Fuck! Damn. Sorry," says Jonathon, hastily standing up again. "Bloody cabbage doesn't agree with me." His obvious embarrassment throws Suzi into unstoppable laughter.

"Sorry," she says, wiping a tear from her eye.

"I can't believe it. I so wanted it to be the most romantic proposal ever. I've been waiting all week for just the right moment, and now this happens." As he was speaking, Jonathon throws his arms up, emphasizing his distress. In the swing he suddenly openes his hand too much and the ring goes shooting across the deck.

"Fuuuuuuuck!" he screeches, as he dives after it.

"Oh my God," yells Suzi, as she suddenly has visions of him falling headfirst over the railings. Jonathon skids several feet then drops his entire body over the ring to stop it rolling over the edge. The laughter suddenly completely gone, Suzi rushes over to him.

"Are you okay?" she asks, bending down. Jonathon fishes under his torso for a moment and then produces the most beautiful, 'cor-blimey' diamond ring she's ever seen.

"Skydiving Suzi, will you marry me?" Jonathon asks, from his prostrate position. She doesn't know whether to laugh or cry.

"Will you?" he asks, very softly.

"Yes," she answers, "yes, and a million times, yes." He gets up quickly, slipping the ring onto her finger before raising her hand and planting a tender kiss in her palm.

"I'm yours forever, Suzi." Now the tears roll down the side of her cheeks as she is overcome with a belief, that he will indeed, always love her.

"Thank you, it's so beautiful," she says.

"And you'll always love me?" he asks, with fake concern. She laughs.

"Until they wheel me away in my coffin." It's the answer he wanted. He grabs her, and with a smouldering passion, draws her tightly against him, as his lips seek hers. After a few minutes of being lost in each other, Jonathon pulls back and takes hold of her hand.

"Come on. I want you in bed now!"

"Oh, I do love it when you get all masterful, Mr Dennington." He squeezes her hand tight and speeds up their walk. Suzi brings up her hand to look at the ring as they hurry back.

"I do love the ring, it's so beautiful. I'm awfully glad you managed to get it before it went overboard."

"So am I. I might have a bob or two but I can tell you if the ring had gone all Titanic on me and disappeared into the ocean I would have gone green."

"Did it cost that much money?" Suzi asks, looking at the ring, suddenly not too sure she wanted it. Jonathon came to a stop and turned Suzi around to look at him.

"Before you get to thinking that you can't possible keep it in case you lose it, I want you to know; you are the most wonderful, special lady in the entire world, and you deserve a special ring." Suzi had a lump in her throat. She had no idea, at all, why she had got so lucky and met her prince charming.

"I love you." And she means it, with every part of her.

Chapter 22

September 2008

Alix and the heartbreaker

Who is louder, Barbara or myself? I don't know and I don't care, the portable player is turned up full-blast and I am screeching out, "I am a woman in love, and I do anything, to get you into my world, and hold you within." I stir the hollandaise, pondering. "Right enough of that melancholy," I spin around and hit the 'next' button on the player. As I turn back to the cooker, Whitney's voice fills the kitchen. "If I should stay, I would only be in your way." Before she can finish the line 'so I'll go,' I spin around and hit 'next' with force. Anastasia starts singing, "Now baby come on, don't claim that love you never let me feel."

Yeah, much more like it. I pick up the wooden spoon and start singing at it with passion. "I'm outta love, set me free and let me out this misery." I flick off the gas under the pan, so I can fully concentrate on venting out my frustration. Takes a long time to prepare tea, as it's dance one, peel one, dance one, slice one. Yet eventually dinner is all prepared and I head upstairs to get ready.

After applying lipstick, I stand back and look at myself in the mirror. I have lost a lot of weight in the past couple of years, thanks to early morning swims and regurgitating evening meals. Although I am aging, in myself I feel like this is the best I have ever looked in my life. Having no double chin makes all the difference. I'm wearing a pretty spotted brown dress that has buttons down the front, for easy access. Underneath the dress, is brand new, pink-satin lingerie, with suspenders holding up silky sheen stockings. On my feet are high heels and all over my body a brief touch of Angels and Demons perfume.

I go downstairs to check for the hundredth time that everything is perfect. The dining table is set for two, candles are the only light in the room and my favourite music is playing softly in the background. *Okay, all done here.* I go into the kitchen and with a shaky hand pour myself another glass of wine. "Here's to decisions." I say out loud and lift my glass to an imaginary partner.

I check the oven, the salmon's done so I switch it off. Everything is ready. I look at the clock it is quarter to seven, I'd asked Pete to come at seven and I knew he would be on time. I open the backdoor and stand there letting the cool evening breeze wash over me and there it is, the knock on the door as Pete opens it and comes inside. As usual Pete jumps on me, his hands wandering over my body. I push him away.

"Let's eat first." *I have to stay in control.*

I serve up the salmon, new potatoes and asparagus and fill our glasses with Chardonnay. As we eat we exchange our news, how work is going, how our families are, and everyday things like that. When we'd finished eating I look at Pete and ask.

"What is it about me that you don't like?"

"What do you mean?"

"Well, am I too fat, or too boring, not pretty enough or not clever enough for you?" Pete takes a swig of his wine and then looks at me with a detached air.

"What makes you think it is only one of those?" You wouldn't know I had been hit in the stomach because I didn't flinch, but he knows straight away that he's being a shit, I can see it on his face.

"Can I have a bath, Alix, my body's aching and my backs killing me?"

"Sure, I'll get it ready for you." I flick my shoes off, leave them on the floor by the table and hurry upstairs. Mechanically, I pour bubble bath in the flow of hot water and go to fetch clean towels. *Why am I hell bent on wanting to be with someone so callus?* Moments later Pete walks past me naked and climbs into the bath.

"Get in with me?"

"No, I don't want to." I go to leave the bathroom but Pete calls out to me.

"Please don't go Alix, stay here and talk with me." I turn around slowly and come to the edge of the bath, Pete lifts up his hand and I take it and kneel down on the floor next to him. *This is our last night together.* As he soaks in the bath relaxing his tired muscles he pours his heart out to me. I sit and listen and make the occasional comment. He always asks me about myself but I can't talk about myself much, I'm too boring, so I lead the conversation back around to him and his problems.

Eventually, flushed and relaxed from the hot water and the wine, Pete gets out of the bath and we go into the bedroom. He whispers in my ear how much he loves fucking me whilst his hands are greedily touching my body. *This is the last time you will touch me.* My eyes stare into his, *can you see my pain?* Pete enters me gently, pushing himself in and out really slowly all the time his eyes bearing down into my soul. For the first time since I've met him it feels like he's making love to me. I can't stop them and tears roll down the edge of my face. When we've finished I lie there for a moment in his arms. *I can't do it, I love you, God help me, but I love you so much.* In that precise moment, Pete jumps up.

"I should get going," he says picking up his trousers. And the decision is made. I get out of bed and put my dressing gown on. I'm worth more than this.

"Before you go Pete there is something we need to talk about." I leave him to get dressed and go downstairs and sit on the sofa. I lift the glass to my lips and my hands shake, I put the glass down quickly before Pete can see as I hear him come downstairs. Pete comes straight to the sofa and sits down next to me, as close as he can. I look at him, soaking in every line on his face. *Why is life so unfair? Why did I have to fall in love with a lothario?*

I have known Pete for three years now, and he has turned my life completely upside down. I love him so much but what I had so painstakingly learnt was that no matter how much I loved him, he was *never* going to love me back. It was time to say goodbye.

From the moment I had met him it had been fireworks, and from the first time he had made me laugh in the pub I had been his. Every time he touched me sparks fired across my skin and when we were locked together in passion fireworks exploded inside me, every single time, for three years, without fail.

"Tell me," Pete said, gently placing one hand on my knee. I look down at the floor, it has to be done I tell myself. *It has to be.* I take a deep breath and look up at him. *I am steel.*

"I need you to choose between us." I didn't know how he would react but I had played the scene in my head a thousand times and had a thousand different outcomes. I didn't expect to see the sadness on his face like it was now. He withdrew his hand from my knee.

"I can't leave Lisa," Pete answers softly. Slam. One door inside me flies shut. Pete's face shows that he knows he's causing me pain.

"I don't love her," he continues.

"Then be with me," I say flatly. Pete's face reveals his concern, and shows his struggle to find the right words.

"She needs me," Pete is looking at me and I feel my heart beat quicken, I know he's not going to choose me.

"It's not just Lisa, it's all the other people involved, so many depend on me." Slam. Another door inside me flies shut. Lisa needs him.

"Her sister's husband beats her up, I am the only one who can go round there and take her sister and the kids out of that situation, no one else can stand up to him." I look back at him coldly, not moving, not speaking. I am done with talking but inside me I am screaming. *Let someone else do it. I need you. I really, really need you.*

"Talk to me," Pete pleads with his beautiful, sorrow-filled eyes.

"I was forty five when I met you," I say softly. "I had never experienced anything that made me feel so alive, as when you touch me. I know I will never meet anyone else that I feel like this with. This is it: you're the other part of me, there's no one else for me."

Pete falls on his knees in front of me and grabs both my hands with his.

"I wish you could see yourself through my eyes," he says. "You have so much to offer a man, any man would be lucky to have you."

I shut my eyes as the third door slams shut inside me. *I can't be all that, because you don't want me.*

"Alix, you know that I know loads of people, I play golf with some, I go to the pub with others, I'm very close to my brother and to my dad. But *you,* you are my best friend. Do you know how much I trust you? I tell you things that I tell no one else, not even Lisa. God sometimes Alix, when I leave here I feel like I have been to a shrink because you help me so much."

Slam. Slam. Slam. All the doors inside me are shutting with a violent force, like some horror film where the victim is in a corridor and the monster, that is, shuts the doors in front of her as she runs down trying to find an exit. *I don't want to be your shrink you idiot, I want to be your lover, your best friend and the person who takes care of you.*

I look at him expressionless. "I need you to leave now," I say standing up. Pete gets up from his knees and picks up his coat from the back of the chair. He looks at me but I don't look back. As his hand reaches out to open the front door I call out, "take care of yourself, Pete." He looks back at me and tries to smile, "you too, babe," he replies.

For a full minute after the front door clicks shut I stand there motionless. Then I'm crumbling to the floor clutching my stomach that suddenly hurts so much. I rock to and fro slowly and my mouth opens, as I lift back my head and release the pain inside me. I howl

like a wounded animal and sob like I've never sobbed before.
run down my face like a salty waterfall. *I am steel.* But I know it's
no longer true, I will never be steel again. My heart was unlocked
from the cold, steel-clutches of fear, the panic of letting anyone in.
I'd allowed love in, and now I'm broken and my heart in pieces.

Chapter 24

May 2009

The girls do the hen-thing

I am so glad Suzi has chosen a pampering weekend for her Hen Doo. The thought of doing something like a long weekend in Ibiza had made me cringe, not that I thought they weren't fun, but because I feel so old.

We're driving through Cumbria, on our way to the Brimstone Hotel in The Lake District. For two days and nights of the most luxurious pampering, and I can't wait.

I have to admit that Jonathon's pre-wedding gift of our girlie weekend away was extremely generous and although we had all offered to pay him back he would have none of it.

As we drove, and the other women chatted, I became lost in my own thoughts gazing at the amalgamation of greens and browns and ups and downs that are the Lakes. I never grow tired of coming here, if I could afford to buy a house here I would move in a shot and spend my days walking the hills and forests and my nights writing in front of a huge log fire.

As we drive into the Brimstone car park I am in awe. The place is amazing, set in a forest with its own small lake; I can't believe how lucky we are to be here. We follow the signs to our lodge as we're not staying in the main hotel and Suzi drives us into the underground car park. No sooner has Suzi turned off the engine when a member of staff starts walking towards us with a case trolley.

"Good evening and welcome to Brimstone, my name is Tom and I am your host for the weekend, anything you need you are to just ask." I raise my eyebrows and look at the others in disbelief; this must be the most upmarket place I have ever stayed at.

"Good evening Tom," said Polly going to open the boot, "are we the only people staying in the lodge this weekend?" Tom had walked over to the boot and started taking the cases out and loading the trolley.

"No, we have a full house this weekend madam, but as the lodges are spaced out I am sure you won't feel crowded. Have any of you been here before?" We all answer 'no'. As we follow Tom to the lift, he begins to tell us about the facilities. There's a communal lounge, for the guests staying in the same lodge as us. We can help ourselves to free, (well at the cost to stay here it isn't exactly free, so shall we say – at no *extra* cost?) wine, beer and soft drinks all day, as well as a continual flow of tempting snacks – no good if you're here to get fit.

The rooms are like apartments of which we had two, one for Suzi and Polly and one for Sophie and me. They had connecting doors which we instantly opened so that we could go from room to room without using the corridor. As soon as Tom had left, with assurances that we should call him if we needed anything at all, we went from sophisticated ladies to teenagers in seconds, from jumping on the massive beds to running around looking in all the cupboards.

There was a bottle of Champagne in an ice bucket in each room and we wasted no time opening them.

"Cheers," I announce after handing everyone a glass.

"Cheers," everyone answers before taking their first sip of the bubbly.

"Here's to love and romance and a happy ever after for Suzi and Jonathon," declares Polly. We clink our glasses and take another drink.

"Here's to happy ever after for all of us," says Suzi.

"I'll drink to that," I say and we clink our glasses together again.

After a wonderful dinner, we go for a stroll through the woods on a well-worn path before coming back to the rooms and turning in for an early night. We all agree we need some sleep before tomorrow's shenanigans.

Nothing wrong with our appetite, we all tuck into a hearty fry up the next morning before setting off for our morning at GoApe.

"Are you sure this is for us?" I ask. I thought the Land Rover ride, through the forest and then along a narrow winding pathway up the rugged mountain, had been uncomfortable enough (although somewhat fun too). Then the hike through the rough forest terrain left me quite out of breath. Now I'm looking up, at what appears to be Jack's beanstalk because it is so high, and although we have a ladder to climb and not branches, I still feel slightly sick. In front of us stands a wooden framework, much like an electric tower, that we're supposed to climb before being hooked up to, and then released on, a zip wire.

"Come on you'll love it," answers Sophie, with a smile before starting the long assent to the high platform. Before we have a chance to follow Sophie, a group of young adults come running through the trees to join us.

"Hi," said a He-Man impersonator, "Mind if we jump ahead of you? On a mission to complete the course in the quickest time possible." I gladly take a step back, and lift up my arm to show the way was clear and then declare.

"Be our guest."

"Great, cheers," said He-Man with a large grin. As soon as Sophie reaches the top, the group of young people go charging up the ladder with so much energy that I suddenly feel like an old granny. *Maybe Ibiza might have been fun after all?* When I was really young, many, many moons ago, I had been fearless. I had stomped along the highest walls without a care for crashing into the docks below and meeting certain death. Nor even as a teenager I'd had no fear as I had hitch-hiked from Plymouth to Cornwall with truck drivers. After all, who would want me? When an irresponsible parent had let my ten year old son watch Aliens I had stood on the doorstep of a very oppressive man and yelled my anger at him for his stupidity without caring that he threatened to knock my teeth out. But now, hooked up to a wire and with a *mahoosive* drop in front of me, I was afraid. *I damn well hate getting old. I thought this was a pampering weekend?*

I take a quick look down to the ground where now quite a few people wait for our group to move on before they made the climb and realise only shame would ensue if I didn't go for it. *One, two, oh bloody hell, here I come!* I launch myself off the platform. I am instantly glad that He-Man is nowhere in sight as I let out a blood-curdling scream.

Time slows. Suddenly I'm not afraid. I look at the Grizedale forest below me as I swing through the gigantic, sky-scraping Douglas Firs, and realise I'm in Heaven. It is breathtakingly beautiful and exhilarating and suddenly I realised there was nowhere on Earth I would rather be. I was disappointed when the ride came to an end.

I pace impatiently, waiting for Polly to unhook herself at the end of the ride.

"Come on," I say, going from one foot to the other, "I can't wait to get to the next one."

That afternoon back at the hotel, after we had showered and dressed, we hung out in the communal lounge helping ourselves to scones ladled with cream and jam and washing them down with lots of wine. The two really don't go together but after several wines you really don't care that much.

We are all comfortable in the huge chairs in front of the log burning fire and we chat away bombarding Suzi with questions about her wedding plans, slowly getting merry and basically finding everything extra funny.

"So here is a take on men and women," says Polly. "Four women go out to lunch, their names are Mary, Jo, Jane and Rose. As they talk to each other they call themselves, Mary, Jo, Jane and Rose. Four men go out to lunch, their names are Fred, Jim, Carl and Mike. They call themselves, Butt-head, Stinker, Left-hook and Magic-Mike. When the bill arrives the men chuck in equal amounts of notes, and although they would actually like the change, they say nothing and leave smiling at the waitress. The women get out their calculators, to pay for their own bit." We all laugh and I nearly choke on my drink.

Just then we are joined by no other than He-Man, She-Ra and a whole host of keep-fit fanatics. I pull my top out to make sure it's not exposing my spare tyre and wish, for like the trillionth time, that

I had more self-discipline and could leave the chocolate, cakes and cookies alone. *Not the alcohol obviously.*

For a while they stand chatting in the open plan kitchenette and we continue our girlie chit-chat.

"Mind if we join you?" He-Man is wearing a tight-fitting t-shirt showing off his six-pack, and oh so bloody (totally not appropriate) tight fitting jeans that show off a rather large swell. *Bloody hell, eyes up girl, eyes up, how much have you had to drink?*

"Of course not," answers Sophie, and within moments our four becomes ten. Much to my dismay, He-Man perches himself on the arm of my chair and, although a very lively hour ensues with much laughter, I find myself becoming more and more self-conscience. I wasn't exactly thrilled when Suzi invited the Olympian wannabes to join us for dinner, but then it was her Hen-doo.

The waiters were more than happy to join up tables so that we can all sit together. I eye the Hen-doo trivia that Sophie, Polly and I had brought in earlier. When we had spilled the stuff onto the table we had giggled and thought them fun, now I was looking at them in outright horror. Sugared willies, liquorish whips, smutty jokes and a Ladybird book entitled 'How it Works – The Wife', to name just a few.

One of the young ladies spoke with a waiter and a few minutes later five bottles of Champagne turned up on the table. "My treat," she says, as the waiter fills everyone's glass. As the evening wears on I realise that keep-fit fanatics love their alcohol just as much as middle-aged, no time to exercise, women.

The evening turns out fab with sexual innuendo rife and laughter throughout, actually a perfect Hen-doo as Suzi sometimes cried with laughing so much. I look at each of my friends throughout the evening and smile inwardly. They are my pillars of support and strength and I have no idea where I would be without them, I love them so much.

Later in our rooms, comfortable in our pj's, we sit together in one room and chat about the day.

"That Steve, (previously known as He-Man) really fancies you, Alix," said Sophie.

"Don't be daft," I answer.

"He does," said Polly. "He couldn't keep his eyes off you. Why didn't you encourage him?"

"To what end? A one night stand?"

"You're both single adults Alix, why not have some fun?" said Suzi.

"It's not fun I want," I say quietly.

"What do you want?" asks Polly.

"My Pete."

"He's not your Pete, Alix. He's Lisa's Pete," said Suzi.

"I know that, but in my heart he's my Pete, the only man I will ever really love." Sophie jumps off the chair and throws her arms around me.

"There is someone for you out there Alix, you just haven't met him yet, that's all." I hold her tight. *I don't want anyone else.* Knowing I am putting a downer on what had been a perfect day I unhook myself from Sophie and change the subject, within minutes we are laughing again.

Chapter 25

June 2009

Suzi's big day

Surprisingly, Suzi had slept like a log, but she'd woken up, wide awake and sprung out of bed at five am. Joy was surging through her, today was the day! She crept downstairs as quietly as possible in an effort to not wake her parents and went into the kitchen to make a cup of tea. She still couldn't believe that Jonathon was actually going to marry her and tears of happiness kept flowing down the sides of her face.

She hadn't finished the cup of tea when her Mum came into the kitchen. Suzi jumped up and ran into her arms crying. Anne held her really tight until the crying stopped. Pushing Suzi away gently she reached in her dressing gown pocket brought out a tissue and started wiping at Suzi's face.

"That has to be the last, Suzi love, or you'll be going down the aisle looking like you've got measles, not a pretty sight."

"Thanks Mum!" Suzi answers with a laugh. Suddenly Anne is crying and its Suzi's turn to hold her Mum tight.

"Sorry love," said Anne after a while, she gave her nose a good blow and then looked at Suzi. "I am just so happy that you've met someone so nice and that you're happy."

"Thanks Mum," Suzi hugs her Mum again. Just then Chris walks in the kitchen.

"Hi Dad, I wasn't expecting you to be up this early."

"Well it's pretty hard to sleep, when the kitchen is full of sobbing women," he answers, "you'd think you had been diagnosed with cancer instead of getting married, the amount of water that's coming out of the pair of you."

"Oh, don't exaggerate," said Anne, putting the kettle back on. Chris comes over to Suzi and gives her a brief bear hug.

"I couldn't be happier for you, sweetheart."

"Thanks Dad."

"I'm just hoping he doesn't turn out to be another bastard, who has your mother arrested!"

"Chris!" yells Anne.

"It's alright Mum, Dad's right. Rest assured Dad, Jonathon is nothing like *him*. One: Jonathon would never do to me what *he* did, and two: if Mum spat in Jonathon's face he wouldn't call the police and lodge a complaint for assault."

"Aye, let's hope so, aye love," Chris goes over to Anne and wraps his arms around his pint-size wife. "She's getting on a bit too much to be carted off to the nick again," he said kissing Anne on the head.

"Aye yourself, I'll never be too old to stand up for my daughter." Suzi was flooded with gratitude for her parents, she never took it for granted that she came from a happy well-adjusted family, where family always came first and love is foremost.

Kim was next to join them, she came flouncing into the kitchen a picture of beauty. At the age of twenty was much taller than Suzi but you could still tell that she was her daughter, slim and beautiful with long flowing curly blond hair. She had already showered and came in her dressing gown glowing.

"Nan, are you doing us all a fry up today?" Kim asks giving her Grandad a wink.

"No," answered both Suzi and Anne at the same time.

"I've booked a buttie delivery for us love, it will be coming in about an hour," said Suzi.

"What did you order?" Kim asked a bit suspicious.

"Sausage balms galore, don't worry you won't be hungry."

"Well that's good 'cos you know how narky Tom gets if he doesn't get something solid in him," Kim answered smiling and popping teabags into cups.

"Tea anyone?" she asked. "Yes please," came the unanimous reply. It wasn't long before everyone else started turning up, including two flower girls, five bridesmaids and a matron of honour, two sisters, one brother, two sisters-in-law along with their husbands and numerous children, followed by two hairdressers, two nail-beauticians and a makeup artist. Chris looked at the throng of people munching their butties, waiting in line for the kettle, arguing over which music to play and who was to have what done first. "All I can say is thank God I'm not paying for this" he muttered to himself as he sneaked out of the room to find a quiet spot somewhere in the house.

It was mayhem but organised and slowly, slowly the girls and women were turned into a sight of beauty, the two little flower girls spun on their toes in their wedding style dresses and declared they were princesses. The bridesmaids looked lovely in their magenta dresses but without a shadow of a doubt it was Suzi in her trumpet, white-laced dress that was embedded with tiny pearls that was the bell of the ball. Her hair was scooped up on the top of head and cascaded in soft curls entwined with the tiniest pearl ropes. Always beautiful – today she was breath-taking, the makeup artist having given her smoky eyes and amazing contoured skin. Cameras and phone's never stopped clicking around her and her cheeks were already beginning to ache from all the smiling.

She couldn't talk to her Dad in the car journey to the church, she just gripped his hand tight and hoped the lump in her throat would disappear before she had to say 'I do'. She had been married in church the first time round but as Jonathon had only had a quick registrar wedding last time he had requested they do it 'properly' and get God's blessing. At first she hadn't been too sure if wearing a white dress for the second time was appropriate but now as she stood at the top of the aisle and waited to walk down towards her love she knew it was right. White was fresh and new and that's what their love was, she felt her knee give slightly as she caught sight of Jonathon, he was so handsome. She still couldn't believe how lucky she was to have him, her perfect-for-me man.

As they near the church Chris tightens his grip on Suzi's hand.

"Not too late to turn the car around love," he said.

"I'm not doing a run-away bride thing on Jonathon Dad, I love him. I really do."

"I know, but in this day and age you needn't get married, you could just live together indefinitely."

"I don't want to just live together Dad, we both want more than that." Chris lifts up Suzi's hand and kisses it, tears in his eyes.

"Just want you to be happy love."

I do's, confetti, photographs and two hours later Suzi and Jonathon are standing in the marquee as Mr and Mrs and greeting their guests. She kept glancing down at her ring, Mrs Dennington, it didn't feel real yet.

Canapés were served with Champagne and the throng of guests mingled together as a quartet played softly in the background. It was a lovely sunny day and because there were so many children games had been set up on the lawn. Adults and children played croquet, badminton and numerous other games. The flower girls were happily jumping up and down on the bouncy castle and the bridesmaids laughed in a soundproof room as they sang on karaoke.

Alix and Polly sat together at the bar as they people watched.

"They do make a great couple don't they?" said Polly, as she watched Suzi and Jonathon holding hands as they talked to different people.

"They do." I was so happy for Suzi I could hardly stop crying but I was also secretly very envious of her. *Will a happy ever after be mine and Polly's one day?*

"Two down, two to go," I say lifting my glass.

"I'll drink to that," Polly answers knocking glasses. "Shame that Sophie couldn't make it," Polly said.

"Yes, would have been wonderful for her to come but she is signing a contract in Greece today isn't she?"

"Yep, the villa is officially theirs now and they are now happy members of the Brits-abroad club."

"It sounds amazing doesn't it? Can you imagine retiring early and going to live on a Greek island, it's like something out of a film."

"Do you think she will come dancing down the jetty to meet us, proper Mama Mia style?" We laugh at the image.

"Yes of course, the four of us will be dancing and singing all over the island, after a few glasses of Ouzo," I say.

"Poor locals, they won't know what's hit them." For just a minute I have a very clear vision of the four of us dancing around the restaurants dressed as Abba and I chuckle away to myself. "I'd be the one on the beach wiggling my hips and singing, 'does your mama know'," I say laughing. "So are you all packed for your own adventure?"

"Yep," answers Polly. "I've managed to pack a year's requirements into one back pack."

"Wow, that's good going. I still can't believe you're going on your own, you're so brave."

"We've only got one life to live, Alix. Got to live it, we don't get a second chance. Anyway, I know God will watch over me." Just then Suzi joins us.

"Having fun ladies?" she asks. We both jump down from the stools to hug her.

"How are you?" I ask. "Are you happy?"

"I can't put into words how happy I am," Suzi answers.

"We can see that," says Polly, "you're simply glowing."

"I told you this day would come," I said, gripping Suzi's hand tight.

"I know, but I didn't believe you. Sure I was going to end up an old spinster and having to marry you Fluffy." We all laugh.

"I always knew you would find your Mr Right-for-you Suzi, gosh, never knew anyone so determined to find him as you."

"What do you mean?" Suzi asks.

"I admire the way you went out unrelenting in your search. Date after date, some nice guys, some not so nice, but you never gave up." Suzi was looking at me slightly concerned.

"It's a good thing," I hasten to assure her.

"Besides which," says Polly, "you had actually given up looking when you met Jonathon so maybe being tenacious in your search isn't what brought you to him?"

"I think it was in a way," I say, "because if she hadn't been on so many dates to find out exactly what she didn't want, then maybe she wouldn't have recognised that Jonathon was exactly what she did want? Besides, you get tired of all the games when you date so much, so when you do meet the one, you're straight with each other."

"My ears are burning," pipes in Jonathon, who suddenly appears behind Suzi.

"Only good things," Polly reassures.

"I'm so happy that Suzi has met someone as nice as you, Jonathon. She deserves happiness and I know you are perfect for each other." I feel choked up.

"Thank you," says Jonathon seriously, as he bends in to kiss my cheek.

"I also have to say thank you for restoring my hope in finding love," says Polly, lifting her glass up. "Here's to love, and friendship, and happy ever-afters." "Here, here," we all answer.

Last Chapter

Feb 2009

Alix and Suzi walk the dog

I open the front door to find Suzi there, all wrapped up against the bitter cold. "Hi. What are you doing here?"

"Just taking Tootsie for a walk and thought you'd like to come to."

"No thanks, Suzi, I'm planning a duvet day with lots of films and chocolate."

"I'll wait in the car, don't be long I've left Jonathon in bed to come and get you." I smile as Suzi shuffles back to her car over the icy drive way. I shut the door and take the stairs two at a time, suddenly feeling a lot better than I had done five minutes ago. I pull on an old pair of jeans and a rolled necked jumper and the thickest pair of socks I can find to wear under my flower-power wellies. Coat on, scarf wrapped tight around my neck I slip my gloves on as I shut the front door and go gingerly down the drive.

"Where are we going?" I ask.

"Thought we would go to the Carrs, not been there for a while. It's a busy place for dog walkers and they're sure to have cleared the main paths."

Driving was a slow business as the roads were just literally slush. It had not snowed in Manchester this much for years, basically the two foot of snow had caused havoc and just as the main roads had been cleared, it had started snowing again. But I love the snow, it brings out a joy in me. Sure enough, the Carrs car park, on Style Road, was full and the Council had cleared the main pathways.

"I thought we could walk through the park down to Wilmslow, go for a Starbucks and then walk back along the road. What do you think?" asks Suzi.

"Sounds great." As we walk along the well-trodden frozen path we play fetch with Tootsie whilst chatting.

"So how are you doing?" Suzi asks, "it's been six months now, hasn't it?" I start adding up on my fingers.

"Yes, six and half months now."

"Have you heard from him?" I give Suzi a half smile.

"At least twice a week."

"Tell me you're not seeing him again?"

"No, I promise. My 'Pete days' are over."

"Good." We walk along in silence for a while.

"My men days are over actually." I declare.

"No, they're not," answers Suzi, "you'll meet someone again. You'll see."

"Nope, I've decided. I'm done with men. I'm really done with crying as well. I've found another way to fill my time."

"Oh what's that?"

"I'm going to write a book."

"You are?" asks Suzi in surprise.

"Yes. I can't write my journals anymore but what I discovered whilst I was doing them, is that I love writing. I've started a Mills & Boon type of mushy romance."

"Well good for you, hope I'm in it!"

"Of course you are, the best friend who keeps coming to the rescue, wouldn't be a good book without you in it." We stop and give each other a quick hug.

"You know I love you, right?" I say.

"I know, and I love you too. Men may come and go, but best friends are forever," Suzi says smiling at me. "Although, I'm hoping Jonathon is forever too," she adds.

"Yes of course, he's a keeper. Did I tell you I got another promotion at work, by the way?"

"No. That's fabulous, what are you now then?"

"Finance manager, no less, with a great pay rise with it."

"That's amazing, well done you. Oh, I'm so happy for you."

"Funny isn't it, I struggled all those years of being a single mum and now they're both grown up and getting on with their lives I'm actually earning a good living."

"So pleased for you, Alix."

"Thanks. You know I don't think of George anymore either? I finally got to stop the wheel of 'memory-recall' and let it go."

"How did you do that?"

"Every time I started thinking bad things, I would pick up an imaginary baseball bat, then whack the words right out of my head."

"What?"

"It worked. I just kept doing it until the thoughts stopped coming back."

"That's fab. Do you think you can use that bat on Pete?" I burst out laughing.

"No. I don't think so. I think you need to want to stop the thoughts, and I really don't want to forget Pete." Suzi gives an exaggerated sigh.

"But you're done with men?"

"Yes, I can honestly say I'm done with men."

Tootsie brings his ball and drops it by my feet. I bend down, pick it up and throw it along the path. Just as the ball leaves my hand my foot slips on the pathway edge. For about ten seconds my arms flail in the air, as my body teeters on the edge of the embankment. The next thing I know is that I'm falling, and then sliding, down the snow covered slope. I come to a halt at the bottom and burst out laughing, I might be soaking wet now but actually that had been fun. I try standing up, whilst knocking the snow off my clothes. Suddenly a hand comes into my view.

I look up to see who the hand belongs to, only to lock eyes with a silver-haired fox.

"Are you okay?" the stranger asks, whilst pulling me to my feet. I can feel my cheeks turning red. *For goodness sake, I'm a middle aged woman.*

"Yes thanks," I reply, staring into his lovely blue-grey eyes.

"If not a little wet," the stranger said with a smile.

"I'll dry off at home." *Of course I'll dry off at home, what a stupid thing to say.*

"Well, so long as you're okay?"

"Yes thanks." The stranger gives me a smile and turns to walk off.

"Come on Trevor," he calls. A Staffordshire, who'd just been having a good sniff of Tootsie, comes trudging along, his big shoulders rolling from side to side giving him the appearance of exaggerated swagger. Just then Suzi turns up.

"Are you okay?" she asks.

"Absolutely," I answer, watching the silver fox walk away. I turn to look at Suzi. "Actually, it was rather fun." I say with a big grin.

"Excuse me." We turn to the stranger, who is walking back over to us.

"I wonder if you would like to go for a drink some time?" the stranger asks, looking at me. *Do I ever.*

"Yes, that would be nice." The stranger grins and hands me a business card.

"Give me a call and we'll fix a date."

"Sure." With a departing grin, the handsome stranger turns and resumes his walk. Suzi and I start head off in the opposite direction.

"What's his name?" Suzi asks, trying to look at the card.

"Daniel Carlisle," I reply quite dreamily, "he's a lawyer."

"So, your men days are over then?" Suzi grins and gives me a wink. I laugh.

"I didn't say that, did I?"

"Yep, you did."

"Well, I think I might have to change my mind!"

Today I went for a walk with Suzi and met a George Clooney look-a-like. I've just come off the phone with him and I'm going to meet him tomorrow, for coffee. OMG, but I'm so excited!

The End *well maybe...*

Villamartin Square.
Sol Golf Urbanisation.

Murcia
Phase 3
Door Number 23.

Printed in Great Britain
by Amazon